06

A FORTUNATE ENCOUNTER

18

A CLAIRE ROLLINS COZY MYSTERY BOOK 6

J. A. WHITING

To hear about new books and book sales, please sign up for my mailing list at:

www.jawhitingbooks.com

❀ Created with Vellum

For my family with love

A cool October breeze blew softly off the water as Claire, Ian, Nicole, and Ryan strolled under the streetlamps along the sidewalk near the harbor. They'd just left their favorite Italian restaurant located in Boston's North End where, tucked into a cozy table by the big windows, they'd enjoyed tasty meals and a bottle of wine. Despite the chill in the air, they all wanted gelato cones for dessert and were on their way to a tiny shop a few streets away.

"I can't believe I won that catering contract." Nicole shook her head. The evening out was to celebrate the contract awarded to the Chocolate Dreams shop for a huge and important upcoming wedding.

"All the movers and shakers of Boston are going to be there."

"There are going to be a lot of movers and shakers from outside Boston who will be there, too," Ian said. "The bride and groom and their families have contacts all over the country."

"And outside the country as well," Ryan said.

"Oh, gosh." Nicole rested her hand over her chest. "Have I bitten off more than I can chew?"

"It will be fine," Claire reassured her friend. "Robby and I will be with you. We can hire some extra people to help if we need to."

"But can we handle the attention?" Nicole asked. "The scrutiny? The fussy wedding attendees? What if they don't like our desserts?"

Thirty-five-year old Claire chuckled. "When has that ever happened?"

"There's always a first time." Nicole shoved her hands into her coat pockets.

"Just don't faint at the wedding like you did at the food festival," Claire warned with a smile.

"I wish I'd seen that." Ryan, a neurologist who had treated Ian after he'd been hit in the head by a killer, put his arm around Nicole's shoulders.

"Thankfully, you missed that scene," Nicole groaned.

"It was pretty spectacular," Ian said. "Right up there on the stage in front of the crowd. As soon as they announced the grand prize went to Chocolate Dreams, down she went."

"I'll never live it down," Nicole said with a shake of her head, her long brown hair moving over her shoulders.

The two couples stood inside the small café and ordered their cones before heading outside to walk over to Quincy Market to watch the people shopping or going out to restaurants or bars with friends or dates.

"Did you hear about the missing girl over in Bayside?" Ian licked the gelato from his cone.

Claire's skin prickled with anxiety at hearing her boyfriend's words. "I heard Robby mention it when we were working today. What happened?"

Ian, a Boston detective, said, "A young woman from Bayside went out with a friend last night. She texted a girlfriend asking to be picked up at a convenience store in Hadwen because she wanted to get away from the guy she was with. When the friend finally saw the message, she texted and called the young woman, but she didn't answer. She never went home. Her mother is frantic."

"I'd be frantic, too," Claire said softly, her finger

and thumb nervously twisting a strand of her wavy blond hair.

"Has the daughter ever gone off before?" Nicole asked.

"Never," Ian told them. "That's why the family and friends are so upset. Jade has never gone anywhere without telling her mother or sister where she's going."

"Her name is Jade?" Ryan asked.

"Jade Lyons," Ian said. "Twenty-one. A senior at Whittemore College in Smithtown. She was living at home this semester to save money."

"What does law enforcement think?" Claire asked.

"Some think the girl has gone off for a while. Just because she hasn't done it before, doesn't mean she didn't do it this time." Ian took Claire's hand in his. "Others think it better be looked into, and fast."

"And what do you think?" Claire asked turning her head to look into the detective's dark brown eyes.

A frown formed over Ian's mouth. "I think the Bayside area police better move quickly on this one."

"You haven't been called in to investigate, have you?" Nicole asked.

"I haven't," Ian said. "I've got a couple of buddies

in the Bayside department. I'd be glad to help out, if the need arises."

The couples wandered the streets up to the Common and down to Newbury Street where they entered a café, took seats at a table near a fireplace, and ordered coffees. The conversation moved from topic to topic, the weather, plans for a weekend bike ride, a Halloween party they were all invited to attend, costumes, and a new movie they wanted to see.

After an hour, they left the café and Ryan walked home with Nicole, and Ian strolled with Claire to Adamsburg Square at the edge of Beacon Hill where the young woman lived in a brick townhouse. Because of an early morning the next day, Ian kissed his girlfriend goodnight and left for his own place.

"You know the dogs will be angry with you for not coming in to say hello," Claire said to Ian as he went down the granite steps.

Ian smiled. "Tell them I'm sorry, but I'll see them tomorrow and we can take a walk along the river together. Tell them I'll bring my Frisbee."

Claire watched Ian walk down the hill until he waved before turning the corner, and then she took out her key and went inside where her two Corgis,

Bear and Lady, were wiggling and squirming with their little tails wagging.

Bending down to pat them, Claire said, "Sweet dogs. Always such a nice greeting when I get home."

Claire rented a gorgeous apartment with two bedrooms, a high-end finished kitchen, a dining room, and a large living room with patio doors leading out to a small patch of green grass and a big old shade tree. A fence around the space kept the Corgis safe in the private, quiet yard. When Nicole saw the townhouse for the first time, she was shocked that Claire was able to afford such a beautiful home, and eventually discovered that her friend had inherited a fortune when her husband passed away.

Claire, an attorney by education and experience, was employed at the financial institution owned by her future husband, and when he met her, he was completely smitten. Teddy had been forty years older than Claire, yet despite the age difference, the two fell in love and were happy together ... until Teddy passed away unexpectedly after only two years of marriage.

A talented amateur baker, Claire moved to Boston, applied to work at Nicole's bakery and chocolate shop, and the two became best friends.

Something else happened when she arrived in Boston ... Claire's perception and intuition became heightened and she was able to *sense* things about people and situations that others could not.

After changing into soft pajama pants and a matching top and pulling her long, blond hair into a topknot, Claire made a cup of tea, and then settled comfortably on the sofa with a Corgi on each side of her. The three of them were beginning to doze when Lady suddenly lifted her head and jumped off the couch. Facing towards the foyer of the townhouse, the dog growled deep and low.

Claire's heart pounded. "What is it, girl?"

Bear leapt down and stared towards the hallway.

Standing up, Claire said, "You're scaring me. What's wrong?"

The sudden bong of the doorbell made the young woman jump and the dogs barked as they raced to the entranceway.

Peeking through the peephole, Claire saw a woman about fifty-years-old standing on her front landing so she pressed the intercom button. "Hello?"

"Oh, thank heavens you're at home." The woman ran her hand over her short auburn hair. "May I please talk to you. You're Claire Rollins, aren't you?"

"It's awfully late," Claire said, uneasy about

opening her door to a stranger. "Why are you looking for me?"

"I need to talk to you." The woman's voice broke. "Please. I need your help. It's about my daughter."

A shiver of worry slipped over Claire's skin.

When Lady rubbed her head against her owner's leg and whined, Claire looked down at the Corgi and sighed. "Oh, okay." She unlocked the door and invited the woman inside.

"Thank you so much. I'm so sorry to barge in on you at this hour." The visitor was dressed in jeans and a fleece jacket, and her face looked tense and full of worry and fatigue.

Holding out her hand, Claire introduced herself.

The woman shook hands. "I'm Bonnie Lyons."

The name sounded familiar to Claire, but she couldn't place where she'd heard it before, and then suddenly, it came to her, and a cold whoosh raced through her body. "Come into the living room."

When they took seats on the cream-colored club chairs beside the fireplace and the dogs sat down on the area rug staring at the visitor, Claire asked, "How can I help you?"

"My daughter." Bonnie Lyons's words caught in her throat. "My daughter, Jade. She went missing last night."

A shot of adrenaline sped through Claire's veins as her mind raced. Why had the missing girl's mother come to see her? What could she possibly want?

"I heard that a young woman was missing," Claire said gently.

"The police believe Jade just went somewhere for a little while. Maybe her schoolwork had over-whelmed her or maybe, a friendship had gone wrong and she needed some time to herself." Bonnie shook her head. "That's not Jade. That's not how she deals with things. She never goes off on her own. Something's wrong. If we don't find her soon, it will be too late." A tear slipped from the woman's eye and tumbled down her cheek.

"Why come to me?" Claire asked as evenly as she could.

"I've contacted friends." Bonnie swallowed. "My older daughter called her friends. We're organizing a search party. We're gathering early tomorrow morning."

"That's probably a good idea," Claire agreed, still trying to figure out the reason Bonnie had arrived on her front landing.

"Would you help us? Would you come with us to search?" The woman's eyes were pleading.

"Why do you want me? We don't know each other, do we?" Claire asked.

"No, we don't." Bonnie passed her hand over her red-rimmed eyes. "An acquaintance of a friend mentioned your name. She told us you had strong intuition, keen perception. She said I should reach out to you and ask for your help."

Claire's throat tightened. The only people who knew she had an unusual *skill* were Nicole, Robby, and Ian and she knew they would keep that bit of information to themselves.

"Who told you to talk to me?" Claire asked.

"I don't know the woman," Bonnie said. "I only know her first name. Tessa."

Lady let out a yip.

Claire's eyes widened. When the people who knew her secret had run through her mind, Claire forgot to include Tessa Wilcox.

"Do you know who I mean?" Bonnie asked hopefully as she leaned forward in her chair.

"Yes." Claire took in a long breath. "I'll help you search."

2

Claire told Bonnie Lyons she did not have any special skills, but had a heightened ability to pick up on things around her that others seemed to overlook. She explained the ability as a strong intuition with nothing about it being paranormal. Even though Claire knew her skill *did* have a paranormal aspect to it, she did not want people to consider her strange or to expect too much from her. She understood that people in a situation like this might cling to the hope that Claire would perform a miracle for them and she had no intention of implying any such thing.

At first light, Nicole and Claire took the commuter train to Bayside, and then walked a half mile, arriving at the town's high school, the staging point for the volunteers gathering for the search. The school was ringed by woods and fields. Most of the trees were decked out with red, orange, and yellow foliage, but some had already lost their leaves and their limbs stood dark and bare against the slate gray sky. Mist rose from the nearest field and evaporated high into the air. The section of woods ran from Bayside right into the small towns of Smithtown and Hadwen.

The overcast, damp, and chilly morning cast a pall over the huge crowd ... Claire estimated there were about one hundred people in the school parking lot waiting for instructions ... teens, college students, the middle-aged, older residents, men and women, all hoping for a happy ending.

In the corner of the lot, detectives and police officers, many with dogs, listened to two people in charge explaining the day's plan and how the volunteers would be organized.

"There are a lot of dogs here," Nicole pointed out as she looked across the lot to the fields and woods where the groups would begin to search. "Are they looking for a living person, or a body?"

"I heard there are two other search groups who

will be working today starting at different points in Hadwen and Smithtown." Claire tried to remain hopeful. "Having the dogs here doesn't mean they've given up hope of finding Jade alive."

A woman's voice called to Claire and they turned around to see Bonnie Lyons rushing towards them.

The woman clasped Claire's hand and pumped it. "Thank you, thank you for coming."

"I'm happy to help." Claire introduced Nicole and Bonnie repeated her thanks to the young woman.

Bonnie said, "The coordinators are getting ready to organize the volunteers. They're laying out the area into a grid. Each group will be assigned a section to walk. We're supposed to watch for footprints, items of clothing, personal effects like a cell phone or a driver's license or keys, things like that. Have you done this before?"

"No, we haven't," Claire said.

"It sounds pretty easy," Bonnie said. "We all just need to stay focused and pay attention to the ground in front of us." The woman's face almost crumpled, but she pulled her self together. "I'm so grateful for the help. Look at all of these people. We'll find a clue this morning. We'll find something." Bonnie's eyes looked sunken and the rims of her eyes were bright red. It seemed hard for her to stand still, she was so full of nervous energy. "I wish we could get going."

Claire wanted to learn about Jade. "Jade went to Whittemore?"

Bonnie stared at Claire for a few moments as if she didn't understand the question. "Oh, yes. She was a senior at Whittemore. Do you know it? It's small. It's very hard to get into. Jade was thrilled when she got her acceptance. We couldn't believe she got in."

"What is your daughter studying?" Nicole asked.

"Physical therapy," Bonnie said with pride. "She's in her fourth year. It's a six-year program. Jade will graduate with a doctorate in physical therapy. She loves to run and bike and swim. She's always on the go, doing something outside."

"Is Jade seeing someone?" Claire asked.

"Yes. Kyle Vallins. He's here somewhere." Bonnie glanced around. "He's twenty-three. He graduated in May with his doctorate. He has a job in Boston."

"Is he a physical therapist, too?" Nicole asked.

"He is. He works at a sports clinic," Bonnie said. "Hereford Health and Wellness. I'll introduce you, if I see him."

"Mom? When are we starting?" A slim, dark-haired young woman approached Bonnie.

"This is Jeena. My older daughter." Bonnie took Jeena's arm. "We'll be starting soon. Any time now." Even though the woman forced a smile, her facial expression remained neutral.

"I want to get going. I want to do something." Jeena slipped her hand into her mother's.

"I know."

"Does your sister have a best friend?" Claire asked.

Jeena studied Claire's face and then nodded. "Cori Ball. They've been roommates until this semester. Jade is living at home this fall to save money."

"Is Cori here?" Claire asked.

"I saw her earlier. She's in the crowd some-where." Jeena ran her eyes over the groups of people milling about, eager to start the search.

"Did your sister ever go off on her own before?" Nicole questioned.

Jeena spun back to face Nicole and Claire. "Never. I know young adults do that sometimes, but not Jade and not me. We would never do such a thing. Mom would be frantic if she didn't know where we were." The irony of her statement seemed to strike Jeena right in the chest and she raised her hand to her eyes. "I mean.... Oh, mom."

Bonnie placed her arm around her daughter and pulled her close, running her hand over Jeena's long, dark hair. "I know, hon. I know what you meant."

Claire's eyes misted over at the mother's and daughter's heartbreak.

After a minute, Jeena stepped back and ran her hands over her face. "I'm okay. We're going to find her. Everything will be fine."

Claire felt her heart sink. "Before we start out, can you tell me what happened the night Jade disappeared?"

Bonnie cleared her throat. "Jade went out with a friend, Alyssa. Her friend picked her up at our house. They were going to drive around, maybe see some friends, maybe end up at a movie or a pub. She said she'd be home by midnight because she had an early class the next morning." Bonnie paused for a few moments. "Alyssa told the police she and Jade met a few friends at the park across from Whittemore's campus. There was going to be a bonfire. Jade supposedly left the bonfire with someone. Alyssa said Jade texted her later that night. Jade wanted

Alyssa to come pick her up. She asked Alyssa to call her when she got the message."

"Did Alyssa call?" Nicole asked.

"Alyssa said she did call, but Jade didn't answer," Bonnie said.

"Do you know how long after Jade sent the message that Alyssa called her back?" Claire asked.

"I'm not sure," Bonnie said. "I can ask the officers."

A plainclothes officer came up to Bonnie. "We're ready to go. Would you like to walk the first grid with us?"

Bonnie nodded and before heading off with the man, she turned to Claire and Nicole and thanked them once again. "Coming, hon?" she asked her daughter.

"I'll be right there," Jeena said.

When her mother and the officer were out of earshot, the young woman said, "My mom doesn't know this, but Jade's ex-boyfriend has been contacting her lately. They met for coffee about a week ago. Jade told me she wasn't getting back with him, but she was crazy about him for a long time. I wouldn't be surprised if she agreed to see him again."

"Why doesn't your mother know about this?" Nicole asked.

"Mom doesn't like him."

"Why not?"

Jeena said, "She thinks he's a cheater. She's right. I don't like him either. Blake's a charmer, good-looking, a smooth talker. He's no good."

"Your sister broke up with him?" Claire asked.

"Yeah. About year and a half ago. Then she met Kyle. He's a great guy."

"Why did Jade break up with Blake?"

"He *was* cheating, but the real reason was Blake hit Jade. She wouldn't stand for that so she told him off and wouldn't see him again."

"Why meet up with him now?" Nicole asked as she pulled up the zipper on her jacket against the gust of chilly air.

"Who knows? Blake can be very convincing. He told Jade he wanted to talk over a problem with her."

Claire's eyes narrowed. "Do you know what his problem was?"

"I don't. It was probably a ploy to get Jade to meet him. He could really turn it on when he wanted to." Jeena shook her head.

"Did you tell the police this?" Nicole asked.

"I did, yes, but I didn't want to tell mom." Jade

shoved her hands in her pockets. "I'd better go catch up to them. I don't want my mom searching without me." Jeena said goodbye and walked quickly across to the other side of the lot.

"Blake, huh?" Nicole said to her friend. "Could he be the reason for Jade's disappearance? Did she fall for him again? Did she take off with him?"

"That would be an easy answer and a wonderful outcome." Claire gestured to an organizer who was setting up the nearby volunteers into single file, preparing them to enter the field. "Let's go join the line."

"Why can't the sun be out?" Nicole grumped as she and Claire took their places at the edge of the grass and listened to the woman explain the process. "Do you sense anything? Did you sense anything when we were talking to Bonnie and her daughter?"

"Nothing unusual," Claire said. "Nothing you weren't experiencing, too. Sadness, worry, anxiety. Wondering what in the world happened. Friends go out together and one doesn't return. Why?"

Nicole let out a sigh. "We'll find out eventually."

Pulling a knitted cap over her head and buttoning the top button of her coat, Claire said with a disheartened tone, "Let's go look for the body."

Nicole stopped in her tracks and stared at her

friend with wide eyes. "You said *body* ... you said *look for the body*. Do you sense Jade is dead?"

A look of horror showed on Claire's face and she swallowed hard. "I didn't mean to say that. I meant clues, let's go look for clues."

Didn't I?

3

"This morning creeped me out." Nicole sat behind the wheel of the rental car heading towards the South Shore. "I was so afraid I'd actually see something I could hardly focus on finding anything."

Claire looked out the window watching the landscape of beautiful colored leaves shimmering in the glow of the late afternoon sun. "I think most people felt the same way. I know I did."

"None of the searches found a single thing. Did Jade vanish into thin air?" Nicole tightened her grip on the steering wheel.

Claire took the flyer from her bag and stared at it. A young woman with straight dark hair falling to her shoulders smiled back at her. *Jade Lyons –*

Missing, it said across the top. Other information about her was also included, *five feet six inches tall, one-hundred and twenty pounds, brown eyes, dark brown hair. A student at Whittemore College.* It gave the place and date she was last seen and a number to call to report any information.

"How can someone disappear without a trace?" Nicole asked.

"I don't think she left without a trace." Claire glanced out the window again. "It's just that no one's found it yet."

"Tell me again what she was wearing when she disappeared."

"Jeans, a black turtleneck sweater, a bright blue zip up jacket."

"Did you say earlier she was wearing sneakers?" Nicole asked.

"That's right." Claire mentioned the brand of high-end sneakers Jade had been wearing. "They were blue and yellow."

The two women were driving around the roads of two towns, the first was Smithtown, a pretty seaside community about twenty minutes from Boston. Whittemore College was located in the town and was where Jade and her friends had gathered to watch the bonfire. The second town,

Hadwen, also on the coast, was next to Smithtown and was the area where Jade sent a text to her friend asking to be picked up at a convenience store.

"Is this the right place?" Nicole pulled into a gas station-convenience store and cut the engine.

"It's the address the police gave Ian." Claire looked around. "Let's go inside."

When they approached the middle-aged woman behind the counter, her face hardened as soon as she spotted the flyer Claire had in her hand. "I don't got anything to say about that." The woman nodded at the poster.

"Sorry to bother. We're friends of the family," Claire explained. "Were you working the night of October 15?"

"I don't have to answer your questions." The woman folded her arms over her chest.

"Have people been in here bothering you?" Nicole asked with a kind smile.

"Some." The older woman's name tag said *Jean* on it.

"We're trying to find out if anyone working here saw Jade Lyons that night," Claire said ignoring the clerk's protests. "She's still missing."

"I know she is," Jean said.

"It could help if someone could tell us some things," Claire said, "anything at all might help."

Jean blew out a long breath. "I wasn't working. If you want to come back tomorrow night, the clerk working then might talk to you. Not promising nothing though."

"Okay, thank you." Claire smiled. "Can you tell us the clerk's name?"

"Nope." Jean turned away and started to fill in the candy counter.

As Nicole and Claire left the store and walked to the car, a gust of cold air hit them in the faces and they hurried to get into the vehicle.

"It's too cold, too soon." Nicole shivered.

"It's supposed to warm up tomorrow." Claire buckled her seatbelt and took a look back to the store. "Jean wasn't all that helpful, but she did give us the tip to come back."

"Why so tight-lipped?" Nicole started the engine. "I thought people would want to gossip, spill what they knew, or thought they knew."

"Not Jean."

"You think she knows something?" Nicole asked.

"I wonder. Maybe she's suspicious of us, or maybe she doesn't know anything at all."

"Or maybe she knows a thing or two, but doesn't

want to share." Nicole pulled onto the main street. "Where to now?"

"Want to drive around these streets for a while?" Claire asked. "Get a feel for the area?"

"Sure." Nicole started chattering about the upcoming wedding contract and the expansion of the chocolate shop. "I could never have done this without you. I could never afford to expand. I'm so glad we're partners now. It means so much to me."

"Me, too. The money of mine sitting in the bank needs to get used for something good. I wouldn't have had the chance to invest like this if I hadn't answered your ad looking for a baker." Claire chuckled. "Now look at us."

"Our partnership is great for both of us," Nicole said. "No one ever knows what's just around the corner."

A dog darted out from a yard and dashed in front of the car causing Nicole to slam on the brakes and the auto to skid a little to the side.

"Whoa." Claire's hands were planted firmly on the dashboard. "That was close. Lucky dog."

"Like I said," Nicole looked at her friend out of the corner of her eye. "No one knows what's just around the corner."

"Literally." Claire shook her head.

Nicole touched the gas and was straightening the car out so they could move forward when Claire pointed across the street. "Look over there."

"Where?"

"In the corner of that yard with the big house being worked on," Claire said.

"It's an old Victorian," Nicole said. "It looks like they've got a big job ahead of them."

"In the corner. There's a dumpster."

"So?" Nicole didn't understand why Claire would point out a dumpster, then a second later she swerved the car to the side of the road. "Do you *sense* something?"

The October light had nearly faded away causing the trees' long shadows to spread out over the yards.

Claire's eyes were pinned on the big metal container. "I don't know. Let's go walk around that dumpster."

"Oh, no." Nicole cut the engine and then they got of the car and walked to the house being renovated.

No one was around. The workers had left for the day.

"If someone picked Jade up at the convenience store and drove around for a while with her, they might very well have come past here," Claire said as she stepped gingerly around the dumpster. She knocked on the side of the tall, metal container trying to get a sense of how full it was. "I'm going to climb up to the top."

"Do you think that's a good idea?" Nicole had her arms wrapped around herself. "What if there's something in there?"

Claire turned to her friend with a half-smile. "I'm pretty sure things have been tossed inside. We won't know if there's anything relevant to Jade's disappearance unless we look."

A frown formed on Nicole's face, but she nodded her head. "Do you want me to climb up there, too?"

"Would you?" Claire asked. "It might be better to have two sets of eyes on the contents."

There were metal jut-outs on sides of the dumpster about the size of two-by-fours which allowed helpful footholds and handholds for the young women to reach the top.

"There's a lot of construction debris." Nicole narrowed her eyes as she scanned the contents.

"Luckily, that streetlamp is shining right into the dumpster." Claire moved her feet over a horizontal jut-out so she could get a better look inside.

Old tiles, sheets of linoleum, wallboard, an old

kitchen countertop, and cheap cabinets had been tossed into the container in a jumble.

"Thankfully, it's just stuff." Nicole breathed a sigh of relief. "I was worried we'd find ... a body."

Staring at the piles of material, something caught Claire's eye and she squinted trying to make out what it was. Swinging her leg over the side, she prepared to jump down into the dumpster.

Alarmed, Nicole raised her voice. "What are you doing? Don't go in there."

"I see something by the cabinets." Claire let herself drop gently into the debris and pushing over the items, she squatted to get a look at something tucked under a broken sheet of wallboard.

Reaching into her jacket for her leather gloves, Claire slipped them on, and with her heart sinking, she lifted something up with one hand. "Look."

Nicole blinked. "A shoe?"

"An athletic shoe." Claire stood, still holding the sneaker. "It's the brand Jade wore on the night she disappeared. It's the same colors, too."

Nicole let out a groan. "No one's in there, right? Jade's not...."

"No, she's not." Lifting boards and tiles, Claire searched around looking for the matching shoe. "Here's the other one."

"Oh, no. Come out of there," Nicole said with sadness in her voice.

Claire told Nicole to put on her gloves so she wouldn't transfer fingerprints to the objects, and then she slowly tossed each sneaker up to her friend.

Before stepping down off the dumpster, Nicole dropped the shoes to the grass.

Claire climbed to the top of the debris at the other end of the container and then swung her leg over and used the jut-outs to move down to the ground.

She and Nicole stood staring at the shoes.

"They must belong to Jade," Nicole said with a sigh. "Same brand, same colors. It can't be a coincidence. What does it mean? It doesn't have to mean something bad, does it?"

Anxiety rushed through Claire making her feel ill. "Well, I don't think it means anything good."

"There could be a reason those shoes got tossed into the dumpster." Nicole tried to grab at straws.

Claire turned her eyes to her friend. "Can you think of one?"

Nicole's shoulders drooped. "How did you know to look in there?"

"I thought whoever was with Jade could easily have driven past here after leaving the convenience store." Claire reached up and twisted a long strand of her curly hair around her gloved finger. "It was just logical thinking."

"It wasn't a feeling?"

"I guess that could have been mixed in with the logical thinking," Claire admitted.

"What should we do?" Nicole asked. "Should we call Bonnie Lyons? Should we call the Bayside Police Department?"

Headlights shined into the yard as a vehicle pulled to a stop at the curb.

The passenger side window slid down and a man's voice spoke from inside the car. "Evening, ladies. Can I help you with anything?"

It was a squad car belonging to the town of Hadwen.

"Yes," Claire said to the officer and gestured to the shoes on the grass. "We found something."

4

Nicole had her hand on the side of her face as she looked at the wood studs outlining where the wall would go. "This is going to be incredible."

Claire had a wide smile on her face as she listened to the head of the construction team point out where things would be located.

"This wall will separate the additional seating area that will tie in with the existing shop's tables," the man told them. "The catering kitchen will be to this side which will become part of the kitchen you're using now. There will be a row of glass cases right here. In about a week, we'll break through this wall and the two spaces will become one and then we'll complete the finish work. Some of the work will be done at night so it won't impact the chocolate shop's customers."

"It's great. Better than we ever expected," Claire said to the man.

Robby, the shop's part-time employee opened the door and stuck his head inside. "Can I come see?"

Nicole hurried to the young man and tugged his arm pulling him inside. "Look at this. Isn't it great?" She led Robby on a short tour of the addition to the chocolate shop.

"It's going to be fabulous." Robby stood in the center of the room and turned in a circle. "You know ... I'm still waiting to be brought in as a partner in this venture." He looked to Nicole.

The brown-haired woman flapped her hand in the air. "Don't look at me. Talk to Claire. She's the one with the money."

Robby eyed his blond co-worker. "Claire?"

"You need to talk to Nicole. She was the original owner."

"Why do I feel like I'm getting the runaround?" Robby turned to the head of construction. "Do you have any advice for me?"

The owner of the construction business stroked his chin. "Think about what unique and valuable thing you can bring to the operation. What can't they do without you? What can you do better than anyone else? Work on the answers to those questions and you'll be golden."

Robby nodded. "I'll start working on my presentation. I might even sing part of it."

"More power to you." The construction head high-fived Robby.

When they returned to the chocolate shop's kitchen to prepare the store for the morning rush, Robby took a cake from the cooler and began to cut it into slices. "Tell me what happened yesterday when you left to drive around those two towns."

"We were in the car going up and down the streets," Nicole said, "All of a sudden, Claire told me to stop. She wanted to investigate a dumpster that was set in the front yard of a Victorian house being renovated." Nicole slipped a pan of muffins into the oven.

"A dumpster?" Robby held the knife over the cake. "You two go above and beyond the call of duty. So was Clairvoyant Claire correct? Was there anything of importance inside?"

"Claire climbed into it," Nicole said.

Robby raised an eyebrow and teased. "I hope you showered after that."

"I did," Claire reassured him. "Don't you want to know what we found?"

"Well, since they're renovating a house on the property, probably nothing but old wood and broken up cabinets." Robby set the slices of cake on a tray.

"Shoes," Nicole said. "Athletic shoes."

Robby stared at his boss. "And?"

Nicole watched for Robby's reaction. "They most likely belong to Jade Lyons."

The young man almost dropped the knife he was holding. "No way." He looked at Claire. "You're kidding. You found the missing girl's shoes? Her sneakers? She was wearing those shoes on the night she disappeared?"

"Supposedly," Claire said. "We haven't heard for sure if they belonged to Jade."

"Who else could they belong to?" Robby asked. "A pair of sneakers matching the description of the missing young woman's shoes were tossed into a dumpster. I can't believe you found them. This is amazing. This is big news." The music school student's jaw dropped as a look of horror washed over his face. "Wait. Does this mean the girl is dead?"

"Not necessarily," Claire said.

Robby and Nicole exchanged a look.

"Why would Jade remove her shoes and throw them in a dumpster?" Robby asked gently.

"It could happen," Claire said. "Maybe she and whoever she was with were playing around. Teasing each other, running in people's front yards. Maybe they'd had a few beers. You know, hijinks, nonsense, playfulness. It's possible, isn't it?"

"Possible, yes," Robby said. "Likely, no."

Claire trained her eyes on Robby. "Why not?"

Seeing the sadness in his co-worker's face, Robby tried to hide his doubtful mindset from her. "You're right. I'm being a pain. What you described could have happened. Maybe Jade was with some guy she'd fallen for. They were flirting with each other. They stopped in front of that house and started to play around, chase each other. Maybe they decided to leave town together for a while."

Claire poured batter into a loaf pan. "You don't for one minute believe a word of what you're saying ... but thanks for saying it anyway. I intend to cling to hope a little while longer."

"Where are the sneakers now?" Robby asked. "Did you bring them to the police?"

Claire explained how a Hadwen police officer pulled up and asked them what they were doing standing by the dumpster. "By now, the police must have asked Bonnie Lyons if those shoes belonged to her daughter. I hope she said no."

"Jade must have been in a car with someone she knows," Robby guessed. "Let's talk about suspects. Did Mrs. Lyons tell you anything about her daughter's friends or boyfriends?" Robby loved true crime shows and internet websites where citizens shared information with one another to try and solve cold cases. "Was she depressed? Worried about anything? Overly stressed?"

"Bonnie didn't say anything about that kind of thing," Claire said as she wiped flour from her hand onto her apron. "She did talk to us about a boyfriend and her friends. Jade went out with a friend to a bonfire across from the college campus. Jade left with someone and the friend later got a text from her asking if she would come pick Jade up in Hadwen. When the friend called Jade, she didn't answer."

"Does the friend know who Jade was with?" Robby asked.

"We don't know yet," Nicole answered.

"What about a boyfriend?" Robby questioned.

Claire nodded. "There's a boyfriend. His name is Kyle Vallins. The mother and sister seem to like him.

He graduated last May and has a job in Boston as a physical therapist."

"Had there been any trouble between Jade and Kyle?"

"No one mentioned anything about that," Claire said. "Bonnie seemed to imply they were happy together and getting along fine."

"Would Jade go riding around with someone she'd just met?" Robby narrowed his eyes hoping that wouldn't be the case. "There are a lot of nuts out there. Let's hope she kept her wits about her and didn't make a foolish choice."

"Jade's sister told us that an old boyfriend of Jade's had recently got in contact with her again," Nicole said. "It seems she met him for coffee. She broke up with him about two years ago because he hit her."

"He hit her?" Robby's eyes flashed with anger. "Why meet up with him after he'd done that? She should never speak to him again, let alone get together with him. I'm worried Jade isn't making good decisions. I think you need to talk to this woman's friends. Get them to talk to you. Figure out what Jade was thinking."

A knock on the shop's front door caused the conversation to pause.

"Who could be knocking this early?" Nicole went to the doorway into the front of the store, saw who was standing outside peeking in, and before going to unlock the door, called back, "It's Tessa."

Claire went out to see why their friend had come to the shop before it opened.

"You're not angry with me for giving your name to Bonnie Lyons?" Tessa Wilcox asked. In her late fifties or early sixties, the woman had auburn hair and dark brown eyes and was wearing a colorful dress and an orange cardigan. Tessa used Tarot cards to give readings and worked with clients who wished for guidance. She had many friends with paranormal abilities and had helped Claire to better understand her newly-developing skill.

"Of course not." Claire prepared a latte and brought it to the table where Tessa had taken a seat.

"I thought you might be able to help her." Tessa sipped the warm liquid and sighed. "The early part of a disappearance is crucial. The longer it goes on, well...." She moved her hand around. "The outcome often isn't good. I thought if you talked to Mrs. Lyons, you might sense something."

Nicole told Tessa about finding the sneakers the previous evening.

"Oh, my. Oh, dear." Tessa looked out the window.

"I was hopeful the young woman went off for a few days with a new boyfriend." She looked at Claire and Nicole. "I fear the worst."

Tessa's words ran cold down Claire's spine and she said, "Maybe the shoes don't belong to Jade."

"Will you continue to help if Mrs. Lyons asks you to?" Tessa asked.

Claire nodded. "I could never abandon the woman."

Tessa cleared her throat and gripped her mug. "I don't think you'll find Jade alive."

A little gasp escaped from Nicole's throat.

Claire clasped her hands in her lap as her heart pounded like a drum.

"Your work will focus on finding the young woman's body, and helping to find the person who is responsible." Tessa looked down at her coffee. "I'm sorry to be so blunt, but I believe this is the reality of the situation."

"Poor Mrs. Lyons," Nicole managed to squeeze the words from her tight throat.

Claire blinked away the moisture gathering in her eyes. "I think Bonnie already knows. I think her goal is to bring Jade home." The muscles in Claire's face tightened. "And to find her daughter's killer."

5

The late afternoon turned chilly despite the sun shining bright in a clear blue sky. Claire and Ian jogged around the periphery of the Boston Common as Bear and Lady chased after them and occasionally stopped to play in the grass with a few other dogs. The Corgis were careful to keep the two runners in their sights.

"Tessa thinks Jade Lyons is dead." Claire ran alongside her boyfriend as they made their way up Tremont Street.

"What do you think?" Ian asked, being sure to keep an even stride while running up the slight hill.

"I think I've felt the same way from the beginning." Claire moved easily beside Ian over the hard sidewalk. "I think I've felt Jade was gone since the first time I talked to Bonnie Lyons."

"It doesn't look good for the young woman," Ian agreed. "It's been days and no sign of her."

"Except for those shoes Nicole and I found," Claire pointed out.

"The investigators concluded that the sneakers belonged to Jade," Ian said.

The two runners moved down Beacon Street and took a left on Charles when the Corgis came charging down the hill on the Common to run parallel to the couple.

Claire and Ian called to the dogs and their little tails pumped back and forth as they ran and jumped and play-nipped each other.

"Those are the two happiest dogs I've ever known." Ian smiled as he shook his head.

"Their personalities are infectious," Claire said, a wide grin on her face.

When the young people slowed to a walk and kept going around the Common to cool down, the dogs took off again up the hill to greet a Great Dane and a beagle.

"Is there any other news on the case from your law enforcement friends?" Claire asked.

Ian looked at her out of the corner of his eye.

"You know I'm not supposed to share that information with anyone."

"That means there isn't anything new." Claire ran her arm over her forehead to brush away some perspiration and her comment caused Ian to laugh.

"I guess you know me too well," he said.

Slipping her arm through Ian's, Claire smiled. "I have very strong intuition, you know."

"I'd forgotten that important fact." Ian put his hand over his girfriend's. "I need to be careful because I can't fool you about anything."

"Have the police been focusing on the Hadwen area? Is that where they're looking for Jade?" Claire tried to find out some new information.

"Hadwen, yes," Ian said. "Other places, too."

"Smithtown," Claire said.

"Yes," Ian told her. "And Bayside as well."

"Is there anyone in the family who could be a suspect?" Claire asked.

"The mom and sister were where they said they were during the time of the disappearance and into the morning. The sister, Jeena, lives in New York City. She was reluctant to go back. She didn't want to leave her mother. But, her job is demanding and she couldn't be away any longer."

The corners of Claire's mouth turned down. "Are

there people who can corroborate their stories? It's not just Bonnie and Jeena telling the police they were both at home then? They could be lying about their whereabouts."

"Both women have people who vouch for where they were and who they were with at the time of the disappearance," Ian said. "I haven't talked to my buddy in the Bayside police department for a couple of days, but if anything big came up, he would have contacted me or we would have heard it in the news."

"So that means Jade is still out there some-where," Claire said quietly and she reached for the comfort of Ian's hand as they called the dogs to join them on the short walk back to Claire's townhouse.

After showering and changing clothes, Claire and Ian heated up leftovers and took their plates outside to sit at the patio table under the twinkling white lights strung between the branches of the tree. Bear and Lady rested in the patch of grass, their noses occasionally lifting up to smell something interesting on the evening air.

Ian asked about the chocolate shop renovations and Claire gave him an update. "It won't be long before the wall between the spaces comes down. It's going to look great. Come by some day and we'll give you a tour. Tomorrow Nicole is interviewing two people with catering experience to see how they'd fit in with the rest of the team."

"Everything's moving fast." Ian sipped from his coffee mug. "Just in time for that wedding contract Nicole secured."

"She's a nervous wreck. She thinks we'll never get another contract if things don't go well."

"She doesn't need to be concerned. With you two in charge of the recipes and you, Nicole, and Robby doing the baking, it will be a huge success," Ian said with confidence. "Are you and Nicole still thinking about doing some cookbooks?"

"Yes, but right now, it's on hold due to the renovation work and that wedding," Claire said. "We also have to train the new people who get hired. We don't want to bite off more than we can chew."

Ian nodded. "Has Bonnie Lyons been in contact with you?"

Claire said, "Only once, after we found the sneakers. She called to thank us. Bonnie told me she was sure the athletic shoes belonged to Jade, but she had to wait for the investigators to give the final assessment."

"Does Bonnie think Jade will be found alive?"

With a sigh, Claire said, "She hasn't come right

out and said it, but other things she talks about ... it's the way she words it, I don't believe she thinks Jade is alive." Claire looked up at the branches of the huge tree. "But that fact doesn't diminish Bonnie's determination to find her daughter and bring her home. I can tell she won't rest until she finds out what happened to Jade. She wants to find the person responsible for hurting her daughter."

Ian looked into Claire's eyes with concern. "She's not going to go all vigilante, is she? She won't try to do anything to the person she thinks hurt Jade?"

"I don't know the woman at all, but somehow I get the sense from her that she'll leave it to the courts to punish the perpetrator," Claire said.

"That's good to hear," Ian said. "It can cause big trouble when someone goes on a mission of revenge."

"I don't think revenge is one of Bonnie's goals." Claire shrugged. "But like I said, I don't know Bonnie and I don't know what she might consider if and when someone is arrested for what has happened to Jade." Claire filled her water glass from the pitcher. "Do you think the person Jade left the bonfire with is the perpetrator?"

"Not enough to go on," Ian said. "Jade and whoever she was with were gone from the bonfire and the outdoor party for almost two hours when she gave her friend a call. A lot can happen in two hours."

Claire didn't want to think about it.

The buzz from Ian's phone almost made Claire jump. She watched her boyfriend take the call, get up from his seat, and pace around the small yard as the dogs trotted back and forth behind him.

The detective clicked off from the call and set the phone on the table. "It was my pal, George, over at the Bayside Police. Some items of clothing, a license, and a phone have been found near some businesses in Bayside. It seems they belong to Jade."

Claire's heart sank into her shoes not wanting to believe there could be more evidence pointing to the probability of Jade's demise.

Both dogs growled low and deep.

"George asked me if I'd come by," Ian said. "Would you like to come along?"

Claire didn't have to be asked twice.

IAN PULLED his car to the curb and parked, and then he and Claire walked over to a man in street-clothes speaking with an officer. When the man looked up, he noticed Ian approaching.

"Thanks for coming over." Detective George Paulsen was introduced to Claire and then he walked them over to the far side of the rectangular parking lot that fronted a series of brick buildings set back from the road. Paulsen knew Claire had been instrumental in assisting law enforcement in several recent cases so even though it was out of the ordinary to allow a private citizen to listen in, he didn't mind that she was tagging along.

Detective Paulsen pointed to the last parking space in the far left of the lot. "It's got tree-cover to protect it from being seen by anyone on the main street. It's tucked here in the corner away from the businesses. Pull in, get out of the car, place the items on the ground, and take off."

Claire wanted to ask some questions, but knew better of it and remained quiet.

"A license was found?" Ian asked.

"It belonged to Jade Lyons. Also a purple fleece jacket and her cell phone." The detective kicked at the ground. "Right here. In a carefully arranged pile, the fleece on the bottom, the cell phone next, with the license perched on top of it. Either someone was careful with the items because of feelings of regret or shame, or he's thumbing his nose at us and at Jade for what he did."

"Odd." Ian imagined the things being left in a stack, one on top of the other, in the corner of the lot. "They were meant to be found."

Claire looked quickly at Ian. She hadn't thought of that possibility.

"Seems so," Detective Paulsen said still focusing on the ground.

Claire spoke up. "Could Jade have left her things like that? Could she have been the one to leave her things stacked on top of each other?"

Ian and Paulsen stared at her.

"Jade?" Ian questioned. "I suppose she could have."

Paulsen stroked his chin. "Suicide? It crossed my mind, too."

"Was she in a pact with someone else to take their lives?" Ian tried to make sense of it.

Looking down at the spot where Jade's things had been discovered, Claire was sure when she said, "No, definitely not. She didn't take her life. Jade did not commit suicide. Someone else put those things there."

6

"When they told me they found Jade's things, my heart jumped thinking it would lead the police to her." Bonnie Lyons walked beside Claire through the Boston Public Garden, past the pond and the carefully tended lawns and the gardens full of colorful mums. "But then I realized that discovering the things probably wouldn't help find Jade and that Jade probably isn't coming home alive." The woman's words caused her throat to tighten and a little sob slipped out as a choking sound. Bonnie used both hands to brush at her cheeks.

Claire's heart contracted and she had to bite her lip to keep empathetic tears from falling. In a hoarse voice, she said, "We don't know that for sure."

"*I* know it." Bonnie's tone was hopeless. "Are you married?"

"I was," Claire said. "My husband died."

"Oh." Bonnie touched Claire's shoulder as they walked side-by-side. "I'm very sorry."

"Do you have any kids?" Bonnie asked.

"No." Claire's long, curly hair shimmied over her shoulders when she shook her head.

Bonnie said, "You're young. Maybe you'll have kids someday ... that is, if you want them." After a pause, she added softly, "If you want to risk having your heart ripped right out of your chest someday."

Under a cloudy sky, the two women walked along the path past the elegant weeping willow trees with their long golden branches reaching down to almost touch the water in the pond.

Breaking the silence between them, Bonnie said, "I'm afraid my ex-husband might have had something to do with Jade's disappearance."

Claire stopped walking and stared at the woman, her heart rate picking up. "Really? Why do you say that? Did he and Jade not get along?"

"He loved Jade." Bonnie kicked at an acorn on the path. "But he has a temper and Jade has a mind of her own. I worry they may have had an argument."

"Did that happen? Did they have frequent arguments?"

"Not frequent." Bonnie trained her eyes on the water. "Mitch is a big man. If he got angry, well, a young woman wouldn't have a chance if he hit her."

"Did your husband ever hit you?"

"Ex-husband. Once." Bonnie raised her eyes to Claire. "I told him if he did it again, he'd be dead by the end of the week. I think I got my point across. He didn't do it again."

"Did he ever hit your girls?"

"No. He knew he'd be dead in a day if he did that." Bonnie shoved her hands in her pockets.

A sense of worry moved through Claire's mind. "Why would your ex be afraid of you? Why would your threat mean anything to him? You're what? Five feet three?"

"Mitch isn't afraid of me. But I have two brothers and he might be afraid of them." Bonnie started to walk again and Claire moved with her. "Sometimes, Mitch drinks too much. It can get in the way of good judgment."

"Could your brothers have had something to do with Jade's disappearance?" Claire asked warily.

Bonnie's eyes flashed daggers. "You think my brothers could have hurt my Jade?"

"I don't know your family," Claire said carefully, "but could one of their associates have had something to do with this? Maybe as a way to get back at your brothers for some reason?"

"No. My brothers stay out of trouble now."

Claire was hesitant to accept Bonnie's reply. "Are you bringing up your ex-husband because he drinks? Do you think he could have hurt Jade?"

Bonnie moved a shaking hand over her eyes. "I don't know. I lay awake at night and stare at the ceiling, thinking and thinking. What can I do to find my baby? Who should I suspect? Is it someone I know? Then I fall asleep and I dream Jade is reaching out to me for help and I wake up and stare at the ceiling again."

"Do you suspect anyone else? Was there anything going on between Jade and one of her friends, or maybe with a young man? With anyone?"

"Everything seemed normal," Bonnie said with a sad sigh.

"Did Jade see her father on a regular basis?" Claire asked.

"Yes. They saw each other often."

"Did Jade like her father?"

"She loved him," Bonnie said the words so softly that Claire could barely hear her answer.

"Do you really think your ex had something to do with this?"

"I guess not." A few tears fell from the woman's eyes. "Mitch loves his daughters. I'm clutching at straws, suspecting everyone. I just don't know where to look."

"Is there someone you want me to talk to?" Claire asked.

"Would you talk to Jade's friends, Alyssa and Cori? Alyssa Pointer and Cori Ball. The police talked to them and I talked to them, but maybe they'd open up to you. They might have some ideas. It couldn't hurt to speak to them again."

"What about Jade's boyfriend, Kyle?"

"Yes, talk to him, too. He might know something Jade wouldn't tell me or her sister," Bonnie guessed.

"Did Jade call you the night she went missing?" Claire asked.

"Me? No, she didn't."

"What about your daughter, Jeena? Did Jeena hear from Jade that night?"

"No. Jeena didn't say anything to me about hearing from Jade."

"Is that unusual?" Claire asked. "If Jade was fearful about something, wouldn't she contact you or Jeena?"

"Yeah, she would."

"So maybe she wasn't in a situation where she was afraid. Maybe she was uncomfortable about someone or something and she called her friend to come and get her out of it."

Bonnie nodded. "That makes sense."

"Jade contacted her friend while she was at the convenience store," Claire thought out loud. "People must have been around, going in and out of the store."

"No one would have kidnapped Jade if people were around," Bonnie said.

"Maybe Jade was in someone's car when she texted her friend to come and get her," Claire suggested. "Are you sure Jade wouldn't go off with someone? What if it was someone she loved?"

Bonnie blinked. "She loved Kyle and Kyle is still in Boston. He didn't take off with her."

"What about someone else?" Claire asked. "What about someone she used to love?"

Bonnie bit her lip. "Jade had a boyfriend before Kyle, but he cheated on her. She didn't want anything to do with him after that."

"Is he around?"

"I don't know. I don't think so."

"What's his name?"

"Blake. Blake Rhodes."

"Did Jade keep in contact with him?"

"No. She didn't want anything to do with him."

"What if Blake got in touch with her recently, out of the blue?" Claire asked. "Would Jade be tempted to meet with him?"

Bonnie's mouth tightened. "I don't think she would."

"Jade broke up with Blake? She initiated the break-up?"

"She did."

"Was she upset about letting him go?"

"Sure she was. Jade thought they might end up together. It was heartbreaking for her, but she wouldn't accept being cheated on."

"What do you think would happen if Blake contacted her and apologized? What if he told her he made a huge mistake and wanted to start over? Would she be open to that?" Claire asked.

"Jade was with Kyle." Bonnie seemed unsure of how to answer. Her face showed confusion and uncertainty.

"Would Blake still be attending school now? Has he graduated from college yet?"

"He was the same year as Jade so he's a senior."

"Does Blake attend Whittemore?" Claire asked.

"Blake goes to Boston University. He went to Whittemore for his freshman year and then he transferred to Boston."

Close by, Claire thought. *Maybe too close.* "I might look him up. See what he's up to. See if he's talked to Jade recently."

"It won't lead to anything, but if you think it might help, go ahead." Bonnie suddenly seemed exhausted. "I never liked the city. Too many people, too much noise. I've always wanted to live in a quiet town by the sea. I grew up in Bayside. I raised my girls in Bayside. We spent a lot of time at the beach, walking in the sand, swimming in the ocean. Even in the winter, we'd go and walk the beach. I never wanted to leave there. But now I've been thinking, what if we had moved to the city years ago or to another state, or at least to another town further up the coast. This terrible thing never would have happened. If only I'd known. Why did I stay in Bayside? Why?"

Claire said helplessly, "Because it was your home."

"I hate the area now," Bonnie said, her voice firm. "I can't stay there. I'll move away one day. Not now, of course. I can't leave without finding my baby. I can't leave her out there." The woman shivered when a cold breeze whipped past them. "Winter's coming. The air is changing. You can feel it, can't you? The dark, the snow, the ice. The cold, angry ocean. It's all just around the corner. Do you remember the year we got that snowstorm the day before Halloween? That was a long, dreary winter." Bonnie looked out over the grass and gardens.

To Claire, the winter still seemed far away, but she knew Bonnie was right. It *was* just around the corner.

"I need to find my girl." Bonnie looked Claire in the eyes. "I can't have her out there in the cold all alone. I need to know where she is. I need to bring her home."

Claire's throat was tight and she couldn't think of anything to say that might comfort the woman.

"You'll help me, won't you, Claire? You won't give up, will you?" Bonnie asked. "The police aren't going to find the clues they need because they don't have this *thing* in their hearts." Bonnie pointed to her chest. "This awful suffering ... like a knife digging into my heart. You won't leave me to do this alone, will you? You won't give up, will you?"

Claire wished she was anywhere else but where

she was ... standing next to this woman so full of devotion to her daughter, so full of such unimaginable pain.

"I won't give up."

7

"I picked Jade up at home around 8pm. We thought about going to a movie, but then we drove around and remembered there was supposed to be a bonfire across from the college in the park." Alyssa Pointer sat across the table from Claire and Nicole in a Beacon Hill coffee shop. The young woman had long brown hair, nice skin, and huge brown eyes. She looked bright and good-natured and seemed sincerely eager to help. "I've been a wreck since Jade went missing. I keep replaying the night in my head, wondering what happened. What went wrong? How did this happen to Jade?"

Claire gave a sympathetic nod. "It's very hard to make sense of things like this."

Nicole asked, "Could you run through the evening for us? You and Jade decided to go to the bonfire?"

"We'd forgotten it was that night. We both thought it was the next week. We got excited about it. It was a nice night and we thought it would be fun to be outside with everybody so we headed over there." The sparkle disappeared from Alyssa's eyes when she realized how the excitement about the evening turned to something else just a few hours later.

"What happened when you arrived at the bonfire?" Claire asked.

"After we parked, we ran into some girls we know from school. We crossed the street and met up with some other people we all knew. There were a ton of people there. Everybody was looking for something to do. There were food trucks parked nearby, music was playing. It was great."

Did you and Jade stay together?" Nicole questioned.

A guilty look slipped over Alyssa's face and her energy went flat. "Not the whole time."

"You split up?" Claire wanted to know more about what Alyssa and Jade had done.

"There were a bunch of us." Alyssa's shoulders

sagged. "We moved around, talking to different people. I went to a food truck with some girls and when we got back, I didn't see Jade."

"Did you worry?"

"No." Alyssa shook her head. "You know how it is … you talk with a few people, then move to another group. Groups come together and then they change. Everybody is moving around. You know you'll meet up with your friends eventually." The young woman caught herself. "Most of the time you do."

"You didn't see Jade again that night?" Claire asked.

Alyssa took a deep breath and shook her head. "I didn't see her again after I went to the food truck."

"But Jade texted you, right?" Nicole asked.

"She did, but I didn't see the message right away."

"How long after it was sent did you see it?" Claire questioned.

"Maybe an hour and a half?" Alyssa pushed at her long locks.

"Did you text Jade back? Did you call her?"

"I texted and then I called. Jade didn't answer."

"What did her message to you say?" Claire asked.

"The police took my phone, otherwise I'd show you. It said, *Will you come pick me up? Call me when you get my message. I need a ride. I'm at a convenience store in Hadwen."*

"Do you know who she was with?"

"No. I don't have any idea."

"Did you see who Jade was hanging around with at the bonfire?" Claire asked wondering if any useful information would come from the interview.

Alyssa said, "She was with her friend, Cori. Some other people, too. But she was with Cori every time I saw her."

"Do you know Cori well?"

"Not well. Sometimes we all hang around together, but it's always in a big group."

"Was anything going on with Jade? Was she concerned about anything?" Claire asked.

Alyssa sipped from her coffee mug. "Not really. Nothing unusual."

"She *was* concerned about something though?"

Alyssa's shoulder shrugged dismissively. "Not really, it was just little things we all worry about, like money and work. She wanted to be living back in the dorms or in an apartment, but she wanted to save the money. She had an exam and a paper coming up so she was stressed about that."

"Do you know her boyfriend, Kyle Vallins?" Claire asked.

"Sure. I've met him."

"How was the relationship?" Nicole asked. "Was everything going well or were there any issues between them?"

"No issues. Kyle is a nice guy. They seemed to be getting along great," Alyssa said.

"Any problems with friends?" Claire asked.

"I don't think so. Jade never mentioned any problems with anyone. Things seemed normal."

"What about any ex-boyfriends?" Claire questioned.

"What do you mean?" Alyssa adjusted her position on the chair.

"Were there any ex-boyfriends in the picture? Were old boyfriends around?" Nicole asked.

"Jade was happy with Kyle." Alyssa seemed to be side-stepping the question.

"But had anyone Jade dated previously get in touch with her? Had she talked with or maybe, gotten together with any old dates?" Claire asked.

Alyssa looked out the window and then shifted her gaze back to the two young women sitting opposite. "Do you have someone in mind?"

"Blake Rhodes." Nicole kept eye contact with Alyssa.

"I think I remember Jade saying Blake had gotten

in touch. She dated him for a long time, but they broke up."

"Do you know why they broke off the relationship?" Nicole asked.

"Not really," Alyssa looked very uncomfortable. "But I know Blake was a cheat."

"He cheated on Jade?" Nicole knew from Jade's sister that Blake had indeed cheated on her when they were dating, but she wanted to draw out what Alyssa knew.

"She told me so."

"Do you know Blake?"

"A little. I've met him."

"Was Blake at the bonfire that night?" Claire picked up a strange feeling from Alyssa.

The young woman's eyes widened and she blinked fast a few times. "I don't know. Wait. Maybe I did see him. I'm not sure though. Maybe not."

Claire looked straight into Alyssa's eyes. "Are you trying to protect Blake from something?"

"Me? No. Why would I do that?" A pink tinge showed on Alyssa's pale cheeks either from getting caught in something or from feeing falsely accused. "I wouldn't do that. I'd tell you if I thought he had something to do with Jade's disappearance." She rubbed at her forehead. "I think I saw Blake somewhere recently, but I'm not sure where. Maybe the bonfire? But maybe that wasn't it."

"Were you drinking at the bonfire?" Nicole asked.

"A few beers."

"What about Jade? Was she drinking?"

"She had a beer when I saw her. I don't know how much she drank. Maybe that was all she had."

"Do you think Jade might have run off with someone?" Nicole asked.

Alyssa sat up. "No, I don't."

Claire was still trying to figure out what seemed off with Alyssa. "You seem very sure of that. Why don't you think Jade would go off for a while? She was an adult. There wouldn't be anything wrong with doing that."

Alyssa shook her head. "It *would* be wrong. Some people might do that, but not Jade. She wouldn't take off without telling her family. She wouldn't do that. Her mother would worry. Jade wouldn't make her mother worry."

When Nicole excused herself to use the bathroom, Claire leaned forward, her blue eyes intent, and spoke softly using an even, gentle tone. "I feel like you know something you aren't telling me. We need every bit of information if we're going to find

Jade. Is there anything, no matter how small, that you can think of? It might seem unimportant to you, but it could be the one thing that can put us on the path to finding out what happened."

Alyssa's lip twitched. "I really don't know." Taking a glance out the window, she watched a bunch of leaves scatter over the sidewalk in the wind. "I was feeling buzzed. Not buzzed, drunk. I think I might have seen Jade walk away with two guys. But, I could be wrong. I had way too much to drink."

Claire's heart began to pound. "Did you recognize either of the guys?"

"I only saw them from the back. They were heading away from the bonfire, towards the parking lot across the street."

"Would Jade go off with guys she didn't know?" Claire asked.

"No, she wouldn't."

"Even if she'd had a few drinks?"

"She wouldn't. Jade was careful."

"If you think back on that night and you picture Jade walking away, can you see anything about either guy that seemed familiar?" Claire held her breath.

"I don't know." Alyssa's eyes watered. "I want to

help. I want to remember. I want to go back and make Jade stay with me. I want to look at everything and have every detail burn into my mind so I can tell you what happened. But I can't." A tear slipped down the young woman's cheek. "I should have made her stay with me. I shouldn't have let her leave."

"It's not your fault, Alyssa," Claire said kindly.

"I feel like it is." Alyssa brushed at her cheek. "When I talk to the police, they make me feel like it's my fault."

"I don't think that's their intention."

"Why isn't it my fault?" Alyssa's voice pleaded for an answer. "We went there together. I went home, but Jade didn't. We should have watched out for each other. See what I mean? I let Jade down. I'm at fault."

"No, you're not. You were among friends. You both knew a lot of people at the bonfire," Claire said. "There was no reason to think there was any danger. It was a group of people gathered for a nice time. I wouldn't have kept my eye on Jade either. There wasn't any reason to do that."

Alyssa's chin trembled. "Except there was."

8

"Her friend, Alyssa, thinks she might have seen Jade leave the bonfire with two guys." Claire sat on a small stool, stocking a shelf for her friend, Tony Martinelli, a tall, burly man in his early seventies with a full head of white hair. Tony had owned the Adamsburg Square Deli and Market for the past fifty years and when Claire moved to the neighborhood, he and the young woman, and her dogs, had become fast friends.

Bear and Lady trotted past Claire on the way to the little courtyard at the back of the market, each one carrying a dog treat in their mouths.

When Claire noticed the treats, she looked up at Tony. "You're going to spoil them."

"Everybody needs a little spoiling, Blondie. Life's too short." Tony filled the cooler with juices and milk. "Why does this Alyssa person only think she saw Jade leaving the bonfire? She's supposed to be her friend. Doesn't she know what her friend looks like?"

"Jade was in the distance. Alyssa saw them only from the back."

Tony scowled.

"Alyssa said she'd had a few beers, more than a few beers."

"Ah. The real reason for the girl's uncertainty," Tony shook his head.

Augustus Gunther, a retired state supreme court judge, sat at a café table sipping a cup of coffee while reading a Boston newspaper. Without looking up, he said, "If the young woman was intoxicated, her testimony would not hold water."

"From what she told me," Claire said, "I think she was pretty drunk."

"An alcohol-induced impaired mind," Augustus said. "Take what she tells you about that night with a grain of salt."

"I will." Claire pushed a curl from her eyes. "I do."

"And be mindful of motivations," Augustus added as he adjusted his bowtie with one hand.

"Yes," Claire said. "What motivation would cause Alyssa to lie about seeing Jade leave the bonfire?"

Augustus folded his paper. "She might not necessarily lie. Perhaps the young woman feels guilty that she didn't notice her friend leave so her mind conjures the image of Jade leaving the bonfire in the company of others for two reasons. One, she can convince herself that she *was* watching out for her friend, she *was* aware of her friend's whereabouts, and two, Jade left of her own accord which absolves this young woman of any guilt. Jade is an adult and can choose to leave a place when she wishes."

Tony made a face and asked Augustus, "Do you *really* think that's why Alyssa told Claire she thinks she saw Jade leave?"

"The young woman may very well be unaware of why she thinks she saw Jade leave the bonfire. Alyssa's mind might have come up with the idea in order to protect herself from feelings of vulnerability over the loss of her friend."

"So you're saying Alyssa might have made up the fact she saw Jade leaving?" Claire asked.

"Precisely," the ninety-two-year old judge said.

Tony said, "The kid was drunk. She saw somebody leave the bonfire with two guys. Maybe it was Jade, maybe it wasn't. She isn't sure. It might be worth looking into though."

"Just be aware that there might be nothing to the claim," Augustus warned. "Don't take her word as gospel."

"Maybe the convenience store has security tapes. Maybe Ian can find out if the police checked the tapes," Claire said. "Jade might show up on one of them. Maybe her companions show up on them, too."

"What else will you do to help the case?" Augustus asked.

"I'm planning to speak with Jade's old boyfriend, Blake Rhodes. He's agreed to meet Nicole and me at the chocolate shop when it closes tomorrow."

"Do you think the woman will be found alive?" Augustus asked.

Claire breathed a long sigh. "No, I don't."

"Ugh," Tony groaned. "I was afraid you'd say that."

"Your goal is to help the mother find her daughter?" Augustus asked.

"Yes. And help her figure out who did this," Claire said.

Bear and Lady had come in from the courtyard and sat in one of the market's aisle's, listening. Lady stepped close to her owner and rubbed her head against Claire's knee and Claire put her arm around the sweet Corgi.

Augustus stood and picked up his paper. "I'm off to a meeting." He looked at Claire. "This is a very sad business you're involved with, but it is very kind of you to help. Mind your safety, Claire. If you need anything, you know where to find me." Before exiting the shop, the older man turned back. "You might pay Bob Cooney a visit. The man is a wealth of knowledge." And with that, the judge left the market.

"Don't talk to Bob Cooney alone," Tony suggested.

"It's okay. Mr. Cooney and I have an understanding."

In his mid to late fifties ... it was hard to pinpoint the man's age as he dyed his hair jet black and dressed well ... Bob Cooney was a former private investigator who was known for shady dealings and having his finger on the pulse of much that happened in the city. He usually didn't do anything for free and his price for information was quite high, yet he had helped Claire a few times, and she wasn't opposed to asking for his assistance again.

"I don't know," Tony said warily. "I don't trust that guy."

Claire chuckled. "Neither do I, but I'll take help wherever I can get it, even if I have to pay him handsomely for it."

"Leave him as a last resort," Tony told her. "And I'll go with you to talk to him, if you want my company."

Claire thanked her friend. "I also want to talk to Jade's current boyfriend. He's working here in Boston as a physical therapist. From what I've heard, things were going great between him and Jade, but, I've also heard that Jade met up recently with her former boyfriend, Blake." Finished stocking the shelf, Claire broke down the cardboard box. "I don't yet have a feel for Jade, what she's like, what kind of person she is."

Tony started away pushing the small dolly he used to move heavy cartons around the store, but then he paused and looked at Claire. "That's because you're chasing a ghost."

IN THE LATE afternoon when business was slowing down for the day, a slim young woman entered the chocolate shop and when she spotted the curly-headed blonde behind the counter, she made a beeline for Claire.

"You're Claire? I'm Cori Ball, a friend of Jade Lyons. Mrs. Lyons told me you worked here. She said you were helping her find Jade."

Claire's eyes widened and after wiping her hands on a cloth, she led Cori to an empty table by the windows. "How can I help you?"

"I hope I can help you," the pretty brunette said. "Jade was my best friend since we were five years old. I'm having a hard time with her being gone. I can't believe it."

Claire hadn't noticed at first, but now she clearly saw the red rims of Cori's eyes, the bloodshot lines running through the whites of her eyes, the nails bitten down to ragged edges. A low-level anxiety seemed to be coming from the young woman's pores.

Cori lifted a finger to her lips absent-mindedly about to bite her nails, and then quickly put her hand in her lap. "I was at the bonfire. I saw Jade there."

"Did you talk to her?" Claire asked.

"Yes, of course. We walked around together. We met up with other friends who were there."

"Were you together most of the night?"

"A lot of the time. Jade came with Alyssa, but Alyssa met a guy she likes and wandered off with him," Cori said.

"Do you know something that might be helpful to the case?" Claire asked.

"I don't know." Cori ran her hand through her short brown hair. "I don't know if it will be any help at all."

"Did you see something? Hear something?"

"We ran into a few guys that night. They were being fun, kind of flirty with us. There was one guy who seemed to like Jade. He paid a lot of attention to her, joked with her."

"Did you know these guys?" Claire asked.

"From school. We'd seen them around, talked to them at events. They seemed nice. We walked around the park with them, stood by the bonfire."

"Did you get separated from Jade?"

"One of the guys, Joe, he asked if I wanted anything from the food trucks so we walked over to where they were parked. When we went back to the fire, I didn't see Jade, at first. Then I saw her walking towards the other end of the park heading for the parking lots across the street."

"Was she alone?" Claire's heart raced.

"No, she was with the guy who had been flirting with her," Cori said.

"Just the two of them?"

"Yes."

"Jade has a boyfriend," Claire said. "Was she happy with him?"

Cori looked around the chocolate shop. "I think she was going to break up with him."

"She told you this?"

"Not really. It was just the things she said that made me guess a breakup wasn't far off. She was annoyed that Kyle was so busy with work all the time. She didn't think he was making time for her. I think she wanted a change. I don't think Jade was ever really into Kyle. I don't think she saw him as a long-term partner."

"So she was open to this guy flirting with her?"

"Yeah."

"Do you know his name?"

"AJ. AJ Phelps."

The name Phelps sounded familiar to Claire, but she couldn't place it.

"He goes to Whittemore?"

"He's a senior," Cori said. "He comes from a very wealthy family. I used to tease Jade that if she got involved with AJ, she'd be set for life. AJ's brother is getting married soon. It's a huge event. Hundreds of guests."

A light went off in Claire's head. Phelps. That was the family who Nicole had won the contract with to provide desserts for a big upcoming wedding.

"So Jade went off with AJ?" Claire asked.

Cori nodded, her face washed in sorrow. "I didn't see Jade again that night. I haven't seen her since."

"Did you tell the police Jade was with AJ?"

Cori looked down at the table. "No."

"Why not?"

"I didn't want to cause any trouble. If I told people I saw Jade leave with AJ, then her boyfriend would find out. What if Jade wasn't going to break up with Kyle? I didn't want to get Jade into trouble."

"Why tell me?"

Cori's face crumpled. "I thought Jade would come home. I thought maybe she was staying with AJ. I didn't want to make anyone angry. But ... but Jade hasn't come home. I texted her a millions times and she never answered me. I...."

Claire waited.

"I looked for AJ on campus. I saw him yesterday in the Quad. I asked him about Jade. He said he and Jade drove around for a while and then he dropped her off back at the bonfire." Cori looked at Claire and leaned forward over the table. "AJ has scratches on his hands."

9

"You work with the police?" Kyle Vallins asked with a confused expression. "Then why do you work in a chocolate shop?" The young man had an athletic build, short blond hair, and blue eyes.

"No, we don't work for the police," Claire explained as she, Kyle, and Nicole took seats at a café table. "I didn't mean to give you the wrong impression. There have been times when we have assisted the police department with an ongoing investigation, but this isn't one of those cases."

Nicole said, "Jade's mother asked us to look into it."

"Why though?" Confusion still showed on Kyle's face. "What do you know about police procedure?"

"Claire is a former lawyer," Nicole said. "We have some skills in research and investigation that the police sometimes find helpful."

Kyle said, "I see." But he still didn't seem to quite grasp how or why Claire and Nicole helped with cases.

"Because of our success with other cases, Mrs. Lyons asked us to help her investigate Jade's disappearance," Claire said. "We're very sorry that your girlfriend is missing."

"Thanks." Kyle's broad shoulders seemed to slump a little.

"Have the police talked with you?" Nicole questioned.

"Several times."

"We'll probably ask similar questions," Claire said. "I hope you can bear with us."

"You work in Boston?" Nicole wanted to get the young man talking and feeling comfortable.

"I work at Hereford Health and Wellness as a physical therapist. I see clients and lead a few exercise classes. I also do personal training with a couple of athletes."

Robby delivered drinks to the table and then scurried into the backroom, but Claire knew he'd have his ear to the door listening to the interview.

"Are you living in Boston?" Nicole asked.

"I have an apartment with two other guys," Kyle said. "The rents in the city are crazy so the three of us cut costs by rooming together."

"Do you get to see Jade very often?" Claire sipped from the mug of hot coffee.

"Not as often as we'd like and not as often as we used to. She's studying and I'm working fulltime, plus training for a marathon. We can't just wander over to each other's places like when we were living near the campus."

"Did you live together when you were working on your degree?"

"No, we didn't. We both thought it was too soon to do that and we liked living with our friends," Kyle said.

"Have you heard from Jade?" Nicole watched the man's face.

Kyle's eyes widened in surprise. "No, of course not. I have no idea where she is."

"Do you think she's met with foul play?" Nicole asked carefully.

Kyle breathed a heavy sigh. "Honestly? I don't know what to think."

"How was your relationship? Was it going

strong?" Claire asked. "Were things going well for you two?"

"I hate to say it, but I think we were headed for a breakup." Kyle looked down at his mug. "I could feel Jade pulling away. And I wasn't upset about it."

"What do you think was the cause of the deteriorating relationship?" Claire questioned.

"I don't think there was a cause." Kyle ran his hand over his hair. "People grow apart. Jade was still in school. I was finished and working. We didn't live a few minutes from one another anymore. Even though we're not that far away from each other, neither one of us cares enough to commute to where the other person is. It was sad at first, but I realized that I felt okay about it. I don't think we were destined to be together."

The words ran cold over Claire's skin. "Why do you think that?"

Kyle shrugged. "It was nice when it started, but we really don't have a ton in common. We don't have the same mindset about things. I don't think it would work long term."

"And you think Jade was feeling the same way?" Nicole asked.

"I do. I didn't feel the same emotion from her

that was once there. She was busy with other things."

"Had either of you started to see someone else?"

"No. At least, I didn't. I'm pretty sure Jade wasn't seeing anyone," Kyle said.

"When was the last time you saw Jade?" Claire sat back in her chair to help create an easy-going mood.

Kyle's forehead wrinkled in thought. "A week before she went missing. I drove up to her mom's house. Jade was living at home this semester. We went out to eat and then we saw a movie. We had a nice time."

"Had either of you brought up possibly breaking up? Claire asked.

"No." Kyle shook his head. "I think we were both avoiding the subject. Things were comfortable between us, but there was something missing. I wondered if we'd meet up less and less, with more time between the times we saw each other. Let the relationship sort of drift away and then when it was clear neither of us thought it should go on, one of us would say something about it."

"Did you know Jade's former boyfriend, Blake Rhodes?" Nicole asked.

Kyle's face seemed to tighten for a moment. "I

didn't know him. He and Jade broke up a couple of years ago."

"Did Jade bring Blake up in conversation with you recently?"

Kyle said, "She told me Blake had gotten in touch. She met him for breakfast one morning. Jade wasn't interested in getting back together with Blake. Blake had some issues he was trying to work through and he wanted Jade's advice. He was sorry about how things ended between them and he wanted to talk."

"Did it bother you that Jade was meeting a former boyfriend?" Nicole asked.

"Nah. I wasn't worried. Jade had no intentions of going back to Blake. He hit her once and she told me that once was one time too many. She didn't trust the guy."

"Why did she meet him then?" Nicole asked.

"She and Blake had a relationship. The guy wanted to ask her advice about things. Jade liked to help people. She talked with Blake as a friend. She would never be any more than that with him."

"So you don't think Jade had feelings for Blake and when he called, she didn't consider rekindling things with him?" Claire asked.

Kyle was adamant. "No, I don't. Maybe she had an interest in someone else, but it wasn't Blake."

"Were you at the bonfire at Whittemore a week ago?" Nicole asked. "It was in the park across from the college."

"I was up at the college, but I didn't go to the bonfire. I met a couple of friends at their apartment near the school. We hung out, had a few drinks, watched some sports on television."

"Did you go near the park at all? Did you happen past the park where the bonfire was?" Claire asked.

"My buddies and I went out for a walk. We passed the park, but we didn't stop. We decided to walk the few blocks to town and get a pizza."

"Did you see Jade that night?" Claire asked.

"No, I didn't." Kyle used a slightly more forceful tone.

"Did you know she was there?"

"No. I knew she was going out with her friend, Alyssa. They thought about going to a movie. I guess that didn't work out because they both ended up at the bonfire."

"Have you talked to Alyssa?"

"I saw her at the first search day. We only talked for a few minutes. I think all of us who knew Jade were feeling guilty. What happened? Was there something one of us could have done to avoid this mess? Friends were at the bonfire … I was in the area. None of us saw anything. Jade was there one minute and the next minute, she was gone. If that can happen to Jade, it can happen to any one of us. It's a horrible thought."

"Did Jade know you were around that night?" Claire asked.

"She knew I was going to Whittemore to see some friends," Kyle said.

"Did she text you during the night?" Nicole asked.

"Early in the evening she did," Kyle said. "Nothing important. Just a few words. I didn't hear from her after 9pm. I checked my messages to be sure I hadn't missed something from her, but there wasn't anything."

"What did you do after you got the pizza?"

Kyle said, "We ate pizza at the sub shop, then we went back to the apartment. We didn't walk by the park or the bonfire. We took a different street."

"Why did you avoid the bonfire?"

"We didn't really avoid it. We were all tired and just wanted to chill. There were a ton of people in the park. We knew some of our friends would be there, but we only wanted to go back and relax in front of the TV. We were lazy as heck."

"Somebody mentioned she saw you at the bonfire." Claire let the words hang in the air.

One of Kyle's eyebrows went up, but he remained calm. "Me? Maybe someone saw me walking past. I didn't go into the park. If she said she saw me in the park, she was mistaken."

"Another person told me she thinks she saw you and Jade leaving the park," Nicole said just to see the young man's reaction.

Kyle shook his head again. "It wasn't me with Jade. Maybe someone saw Jade and expected me to be there, too, or thought whoever Jade was with was me. I wasn't there. I only walked by the park. I wasn't at the bonfire and I didn't see Jade."

Claire thought the young man's answers sounded rehearsed and wondered if someone had been coaching him in how to respond to certain inquiries.

"Did you go home that night or did you stay over with your friends?" Claire asked.

"I went home," Kyle said.

"Is there anyone who can vouch for that?" Nicole asked.

"My buddies can tell you I left their apartment around 11pm."

"Is there anyone who can vouch for you about where you went after you left the apartment?"

"I was alone," Kyle reported. "I drove back to Boston. I didn't see anyone I knew. When I got back to my apartment, my roommates were asleep. They didn't see or hear me come in. So no, there isn't anyone who can vouch for me during the time I was driving home or arriving home."

"Are you sure you didn't run into Jade?" Nicole asked with a firm tone.

"I'm positive." Kyle's jaw muscle twitched.

Claire wasn't sure if she believed him.

10

In the waning October sunlight, Claire and Ian walked along the river each holding one of the Corgis' leashes. Bear and Lady stopped here and there to sniff the ground and the humans patiently waited for them before moving on.

Claire had been telling her boyfriend about the interviews she'd done. "Did you ask your friend, George, if he talked to AJ Phelps?"

Ian nodded. "A different detective went to see him. He reported that AJ does indeed have scratches on his hands and arms. The young man told the detective he got the scratches when he went running in the woods, tripped, and slid into a bush full of thorns. He seemed pretty convincing. AJ demonstrated how he put his hands out to break the fall and ended up in the lower branches of the bush."

"Really? His excuse was believable?" Claire's feet scrunched over some colorful leaves on the path.

"It seems AJ's friend told the detective that he was with him the night Jade went missing."

"That's convenient, isn't it? Did the detective get a sense he might be lying?" Claire asked.

"It's always hard to tell. The young man said AJ was with him, therefore AJ has an alibi."

But Jade's friend says she saw Jade leaving the park with AJ," Claire said. "Was AJ's friend with them then?"

Ian shrugged. "I don't know. That's all the information I got from my pal. Anyway, someone else said they thought Jade might have been with her boyfriend. Some people seem to be seeing things that aren't there, or did Jade leave the bonfire more than once?"

"You mean she left with one guy, returned to the park, and then left with someone else? There couldn't have been time for all that." Claire let out a groan. "There are three options. People are either mistaken, lying, or telling the truth about what they saw. How will we figure it out?"

"More investigation," Ian said with a smile. "Has

Mrs. Lyons been in contact with you?"

"Yes." Claire sighed. "I feel like I'm failing her. She was so hopeful I would be able to help. My intuition must be on vacation because I'm not getting strong feelings one way or the other."

"Give it time." Ian took her hand as they rounded a bend on the pathway. "George and another detective talked to the clerk at the convenience store. She was on-duty the night Jade disappeared. She wasn't much help, claimed she really didn't remember Jade coming in. Even though she recognized Jade's photograph, she claims to have no memory of what Jade bought or did. The clerk said it was a very busy night in the store."

"That's too bad. Nicole and I were going to go talk to the clerk, but we were tied up that night. Dead ends everywhere."

Bear turned his head to his owner and barked.

Ian chuckled. "Bear has something to say."

"I wish I could understand him because he often seems to know things," Claire said as she zipped her jacket against the cooler air.

"Maybe Bear has some skills like his owner has," Ian said. "Anyway, George suggested you and Nicole might want to take a ride over to the convenience store in Hadwen and talk to the clerk. He said she seemed to clam up when they talked to her and maybe she'd be more open with two young women who aren't members of law enforcement."

Claire looked out over the river. The water was choppy and looked slate gray. "We can do that. We've actually been meaning to go back to that store. I don't know if it will be of any use. We don't have any magic to use on the clerk."

Ian put his arm around Claire's shoulders and smiled. "Are you sure?"

THE CLERK LOOKED up at the two young women who placed a candy bar, a small bag of chips, and a bottle of water on the counter to be rung up. The slim, petite woman was about sixty with dark curly hair cut close to the head. A few strands of gray wove through the hair. *Brenda* was written on her name tag.

Claire placed a photo of Jade on the counter. "We're friends of the missing girl's family. They asked us to help search for Jade. Were you working that night? She supposedly came in here after leaving a bonfire in the next town."

Brenda glanced down at the picture. "We're not

supposed to talk about it."

"Management told you not to?" Nicole asked.

Brenda shrugged as she rang up the items.

"Do you recognize the young woman in the photo?" Claire asked.

Brenda looked again. "Maybe."

"Did she come inside the store?"

"I think so. Look, I don't know anything. I don't want to get into trouble." Brenda took some cash from Nicole and made change. "You want a bag?"

"No, thanks." Nicole scooped up the items.

"Did Jade come inside that night?" Claire asked again. "We don't want you to get into trouble. We'll keep anything you say to us private."

"She came in." Brenda spoke softly.

"Was she with anyone?"

"Not at first. She bought a water."

"Then she left?" Claire asked.

"She went over to the corner." Brenda poked her chin out to indicate where Jade was standing in the store. "She used her phone."

Claire and Nicole took a quick glance to the corner of the store that Brenda gestured to.

"To make a call?" Claire asked.

"To text."

"How did she seem?" Nicole asked.

Brenda leaned against the counter and sighed. "I never saw the girl before. I don't know how she usually is, but she seemed sort of nervous, like she wanted to hide or something."

"Did she ask you for help?"

"No." Brenda scoffed. "I think she'd been drinking."

"Why do you say that?" Claire asked.

"I could smell it on her when she bought the water. It wasn't a lot, but I got a whiff of booze when she said thank you."

"So she bought water, but didn't leave right away?" Nicole questioned.

"That's right. She used her phone. She seemed like she might be waiting for somebody," Brenda said. "She didn't seem to be in a hurry to leave."

"Then what happened?" Claire looked directly at the clerk.

"Look, I don't want to get into trouble. I don't know anything else."

An older woman carried a few items to the counter and Claire and Nicole moved away so Brenda could ring up the things. After the woman took her bag and left, Brenda gave the two young women a look.

"I told you more than I should have. There's

nothing more to say." Brenda busied herself filling cigarette cartons into the holder behind the cash register.

"We only have a few more things to ask." Claire moved closer to the counter.

Brenda didn't acknowledge the statement, just kept pushing cartons into their places.

Nicole asked, "Did Jade stay for a long time?"

Without turning around, Brenda muttered, "I don't remember."

"Did she talk to you?" Claire asked. "Did she ask you anything?"

"No."

"As you can imagine, Jade's mother is very upset," Claire said. "She's desperate to find her daughter. She can't sleep. She stays up almost all night waiting for a knock on the door, hoping her daughter will come back home."

Nicole said, "We're only trying to figure out what happened. We only want to find out where Jade is."

"The mother came in here." Brenda's face was stern. "She asked a bunch of questions. I told her I couldn't talk about it and anyway, I didn't know anything that would help her find her kid.

"She cussed me out. She got hysterical. The assistant manager had to escort her out. He told her she couldn't come back." Brenda had a hand on her slender hip. "I didn't appreciate her cussing at me. There was no need of it."

"You're right. Mrs. Lyons had no right to be rude. I'm sorry that happened," Claire said. "Mrs. Lyons is ... well, she's drowning in grief. She doesn't know what to do or where to look. She's in a terrible panic. It's very difficult to be around her. But I'd do the same thing if it was my daughter."

Brenda went back to filling in the cigarette case, but Claire sensed a change in the woman's demeanor.

"The girl asked me if the red car was still at the gas pump." Brenda didn't look around, just faced the shelving she was working on.

"Was it gone?" Nicole asked.

"It was still there," Brenda said.

"Did Jade seem happy or sad that it was still there?" Claire wanted to rush all of her questions in case the woman clammed up.

"I don't know. I told her the car was there, then a customer came to the counter and I waited on him."

"What happened next?" Claire asked. "Did Jade leave the store?"

"A guy opened the door. He poked his head in. He asked the girl if she was ready."

"Did Jade leave with him?" Nicole asked.

"She left the store. I don't know if she went with him or not. It was dark out. I didn't bother to watch. I had things to do."

"What did the guy look like?"

"Dark blond hair. Dressed nice. Tall. Looked like an athlete. Was probably rich."

"Why do you say that?" Nicole asked.

"That red car looked kind of expensive," Brenda said. "That's all I got to say. I can't be talking the whole time. I'll get into trouble."

"Thank you," Claire said warmly. "You've been a big help. Thanks so much."

Claire and Nicole had taken a few steps to the door when Brenda said, "Hey."

The women turned around.

"That rich guy was with someone else. Another guy. He was standing behind the rich one." Brenda glanced around and lowered her voice. "That guy is trouble. He sells drugs. He's a mean one. You tell anyone I said this to you, I'll say you lied."

"Do you know that guy's name?" Claire asked.

Brenda looked through the glass to see if anyone was outside the store. "Badger," she whispered. Then she spun around and hurried to the back of the store.

11

Blake Rhodes was a little over six feet tall, broad-shouldered, sandy-haired, blue-eyed, and exceedingly charming. He greeted Claire and Nicole with a warm smile, a friendly demeanor, and a firm handshake. Claire could see how the man with the easy, straightforward manner might easily sweep a young woman off her feet.

She had to keep reminding herself that Blake had cheated on Jade and had once struck her. It wasn't hard to imagine Blake begging forgiveness with his bright eyes and sorrowful tone of voice promising never to raise a hand again, and the woman feeling guilty and giving him another chance. It wouldn't take long for him to hit her again and then go through the same rotation of ... get angry, hit, promise it would never happen again, be forgiven ... and round and round it would go. But not with Jade. She put her foot down and broke up with Blake.

Until he contacted her again?

In the Boston university student center, a multi-story glass, wood, and steel building with comfortable seating, an outdoor patio, two terraces, an upscale food court, and soft lighting, Claire and Nicole made conversation with the young man asking about school, sports, and his plans after he graduated, before leading him to the main point of discussion.

"You dated Jade Lyons?" Claire asked keeping a friendly expression on her face.

"I did. We broke up about a year and a half ago." Blake smiled showing perfect white teeth. "It wasn't the best match."

"Why not?" Nicole asked.

Blake gave a shrug. "It's hard to pinpoint." His forehead creased as he took a sip of his iced coffee. "It was just the right time to end it."

"Were you or Jade seeing other people?" Claire asked.

"That didn't have any bearing on the breakup." Blake leaned comfortably back in his chair.

"So one of you *was* dating someone else?" Claire pressed.

"I wasn't. I don't think Jade was either."

Nicole leaned forward, her eyes glued to Blake's. "We heard you cheated on Jade."

Blake's eyes went wide before he quickly returned his facial expression to neutral and collected himself. "Where did you hear that?"

"People who knew Jade brought it up." Claire kept her focus on the young man.

Blake stretched his arm out over the chair next to him and cocked his head to the side in what Claire considered to be a slightly challenging position. "Listen, people like to talk, especially about things they don't have first-hand knowledge of."

"So you're telling us that these people are mistaken?" Claire asked. "You weren't seeing anyone else?"

"I wasn't *involved* with anyone." Blake tried to weasel out of the allegation by carefully choosing his words.

"What would you call it then?" Nicole gave the man a look of distaste.

Blake shook his head dismissively, but kept his smile firmly on his mouth. "A flirtation. Youthful hijinks. Fooling around. It wasn't a relationship. It meant nothing."

"What was Jade like?" Claire asked. She'd been trying to form an image of the missing girl in her mind, but felt like she didn't have a good handle on her.

Blake's face turned serious. "Athletic, strong, smart, fun, caring. She loved music. She loved to read. She wanted to know about the world and what was going on in it. She didn't take any guff from anyone. Jade had a plan for her future. She wanted her own business, wanted to open a physical therapy center. She loved the beach in Bayside not far from her mother's house." For a half-second, something passed over the man's face and was gone. He made eye contact with Claire. "Is there any news about Jade?"

"I'm afraid not." Claire pushed at a stray curl to move it from her eye. "We're trying to gather as much information as possible to help with the investigation."

"When was the last time you saw Jade?" Nicole asked.

"Um. Let's see. I think it was about two weeks ago." Blake looked down at his mug. "Yeah, I think that's right."

"I thought you and Jade broke up a while ago?" Nicole narrowed her eyes at the young man.

"We did, but I texted her and asked if she wanted to meet for coffee."

"Why?" Nicole asked in a direct tone.

Blake moved his hand in the air. "I wanted to see how she was doing."

"Didn't you run into each other now and then?" Nicole asked, a little bit of suspicion sneaking into her voice. "We know you spent your freshman year at Whittemore. You visited there on the campus sometimes, didn't you? It's not a large school. When you were there, you must have seen Jade once in a while."

"We'd run into each other sometimes when I was up there visiting friends, but we would just say 'hi' and move along. I got the idea to meet up with her, see how she was."

"Why?" Nicole asked, keeping her eyes on Blake.

"Jade and I were together for a long time. I was thinking about her. I thought it would be nice to catch up. We'd been apart for over a year. I thought we could talk without any anger or uncomfortable feelings coming up. We could just be normal. Like old friends."

"Did you want to talk to Jade about anything specific?" Claire asked.

"Not really," Blake said.

Nicole didn't beat around the bush in her questioning. "Did you want to get back with her?"

"No. I wanted to talk. See how she was doing. That's all."

"Maybe a tiny thought was in your mind about dating her again?" Nicole asked.

"No. That wasn't the point of getting together with her."

"Did you have something on your mind? Did you want Jade's opinion on something?" Claire asked again.

Blake rolled his eyes and let out a snort of exasperation. "I didn't have an ulterior motive. Jeez. I saw her across the quad one day not long ago and thought it would be nice to talk to her."

"Was she reluctant to meet you?" Claire asked.

"Sort of. I told her what I've been telling you. I only wanted to get a coffee and talk to someone who had been a friend."

"You mean girlfriend, don't you?" Nicole asked.

"Jade was my friend, too."

"Were you at the bonfire?" Claire asked.

"No. Some of my friends went. They asked me to come up, but I wasn't feeling great that day so I stayed in Boston."

"Nobody would say they saw you at the bonfire?"

Blake answered evenly. "I wasn't at the park that night so if someone says I was, then he or she would be mistaken."

"What did you and Jade talk about when you met for coffee?" Nicole asked.

"Everything. Her new boyfriend, her studies, how I liked being in Boston, our plans for after we graduated. Stuff like that," Blake told them. "It wasn't any earth-shattering conversation. It was just catching up with one another."

"With no ulterior motive?" Nicole eyed the young man.

"That's right." Blake sighed. "I didn't like how we broke up. I think there were hard feelings on both sides. That bugged me. I wanted to smooth things out between us, not leave each other on negative terms. I cared about Jade. I hoped the best for her."

"Any idea where she might be?" Claire asked.

"Me? No. No idea at all." Blake had a look of surprise on his face. "How would I know?"

"Jade might have said something to you," Claire

suggested. "She might have implied something, like going away with someone for a while, or she may have been thinking about leaving school, she may have needed a break."

"Jade wouldn't leave school," Blake said flatly. "That wasn't part of her plan."

"Plans can change," Nicole said.

Blake nodded. "Sure, but school was going to get Jade where she wanted to be. She wouldn't quit school. That just isn't Jade."

"Did Jade hang out with any questionable people?" Claire asked.

"Questionable? How?"

Claire clarified, "People who might have had a drinking problem, someone who had a drug problem, somebody who only wanted to have fun, goof off, forget about classes. You must know some people like that."

"I don't know if Jade knew people like that." Blake crossed his arms over his chest.

"Did Jade do drugs?" Nicole asked.

Blake sat up. "Jade? No way. She barely drank."

"Would you say alcohol had ever been a problem for her?"

"Definitely not," Blake said. "Unless I missed stuff, which I didn't."

"When you met her for coffee, did Jade bring up anything that was bothering her?"

Blake rubbed at his forehead. "She mentioned a tough chemistry class. Jade was worried about her grade. She didn't like living at home this semester. Not because she didn't get along with her mom. She did, but Jade wanted to be an adult, have her own place, not feel so dependent on her mother."

"Do you know Kyle Vallins, Jade's boyfriend?" Claire asked.

"No," Blake shook his head. "I don't want to know him."

"Do you know someone named AJ Phelps?" Nicole asked.

A foul look washed over Blake's face. "I know who he is. Why?"

"What do you know about him?"

Blake looked like the words he was about to say were distasteful. "He's smart, a good athlete. He also thinks he's great, the best at everything. His family's loaded, and I mean, loaded. I think coming from all that money and privilege has given AJ a sense of arrogance. If he does anything wrong? His dad will get him out of trouble. I think AJ thinks he's untouchable."

Worry pricked Claire's skin. *Untouchable*? Not a

great quality to have, she thought. Especially if someone wanted to commit a crime ... and get away with it.

12

————

"I'm glad you could meet me here. I had to practice today. We have a team in the charity golf tournament next week." AJ Phelps, twenty-one-years old, was six feet tall with an athletic build, blond hair and blue eyes. Wearing chinos and a white golf shirt, he sat in a leather chair across from Claire in the country club dining room eating lunch. AJ had that easy, confidant air of the very wealthy, an aura of being invincible and set apart.

The man was charming and friendly, smiling and making eye contact with Claire, but she had the slight impression that he was talking down to her since he assumed she was not in his financial sphere. Chuckling to herself, she knew young AJ would probably faint if he discovered her net worth and she would have loved to see his expression if it was ever revealed to him, but Claire kept that information private and closely guarded and AJ would never find out.

She'd noticed the scratches on the man's hands and decided to bring them up later in the conversation.

Setting half of her hummus and vegetable sandwich on the plate, Claire dabbed her lips with the napkin. "I'm glad you were able to set some time aside to speak with me."

"I'm happy to do what I can to help." AJ sipped from the glass of iced tea.

"You knew Jade Lyons?"

"I know who she is," AJ said. "Whittemore is small so we know just about everyone in our class year. I guess I should say we're familiar with one another. We aren't all friends. The class isn't *that* small."

"Had you socialized with Jade?"

"No, I hadn't. We were in different circles." AJ took a bite of his club sandwich. "We didn't cross paths very often. We'd been in a couple of classes together, but they were big and we didn't interact much."

"What was your impression of her?" Claire asked.

One of AJ's eyebrows went up slightly and he grinned. "Well, I thought she was beautiful, if that's what you mean."

"What about her personality?" Claire asked.

"She seemed nice, polite, friendly. She seemed smart when she answered questions in class. Beauty and brains, a winning combination." AJ sat up straight.

Claire didn't care for AJ's comments. It wasn't so much what he said, but the manner in which he said them. A trace of arrogance tinged his tone.

"Did you ever ask her out?"

AJ said, "I didn't. Jade always had a boyfriend. I understand the relationship didn't work out with the guy she dated in her first couple of years in college, but then she started going out with Kyle Vallins. Do you know him? He's a physical therapist now. He's a few years older than I am. He did his professional doctorate at Whittemore." AJ smiled and showed his sparkling teeth. "Anyway, I was never quick enough to get a date with Jade."

The lightness of AJ's comments made Claire wonder if he was aware of Jade's disappearance. "Have the police spoken to you?"

"Yes, they did. They told me it was merely a formality ... that they were speaking with a lot of people who had interactions with Jade."

"You saw Jade at the bonfire?"

"I did. I was walking around with a few friends and we ran into Jade and some of her girlfriends. We all hung around for a while, walked around the park, stood and watched the fire."

"Did you talk a lot with Jade that night?" Claire asked.

"Yeah. We were all having a good time. It was a great night. Perfect weather."

"Did you flirt with her?"

"Some." The smirk that formed across AJ's mouth rubbed Claire the wrong way.

"Did she flirt back?"

"She did."

"Had you been drinking?" Claire asked.

"Sure. I wasn't drunk," AJ said with a slight tone of defensiveness.

"What about Jade? Had she been drinking?"

AJ shifted in his seat like the questions made him uncomfortable. "I saw her have a beer. Only one though."

"Did Jade act drunk?"

"I never hung out with her before, so I really can't say."

"You must know how drunk people act." Claire held the young man's eyes. "I'm sure you've seen your share of intoxicated people. I'll be more specific. Did Jade stumble when she was walking?"

"No. I didn't notice that she did."

"Did she slur her words?"

"No, she seemed fine when she talked," AJ said.

"Did you and Jade separate from the group at some point in the evening?"

"We walked in the park for a while, along the walkways and paths, away from the bonfire."

"Did you ask her to walk with you?"

AJ's eyebrows moved closer to together as he thought about the question. "I don't remember. I don't think we made a conscious decision to move away from the others. I think we just wandered off."

"Did you ask her back to your place?"

AJ's face hardened. "I think that's our business."

Claire leaned forward and said in a soft voice trying to keep the emotion out of it, "Jade has been missing for over a week. What happened that night isn't your business alone. It isn't Jade's business alone. It is now the business of everyone who is trying to find her. Your privacy doesn't matter to me. Finding Jade is what matters."

For a few seconds, AJ looked like he had been slapped, but he blinked several times and swallowed. "You're right. Jade came to my apartment. It's right near the park and the campus, only a few minutes' walk. We had a beer, we talked. We weren't there long. Maybe forty minutes. We kissed once. Jade was uncomfortable. She said she had a boyfriend. She planned to break up with him, but she didn't want to cheat. She knew what it felt like to be cheated on. Jade said she'd like to hang out with me again once she'd broken off with the boyfriend."

"How did you take that?" Claire asked.

"I understood completely. In fact, I was impressed with Jade's ethics."

Claire felt a strange sensation move over her skin. "What happened next?"

AJ looked down at his lunch plate. "We went back to the bonfire."

A tingle flickered down Claire's back. "Did you rejoin the group?"

"We walked over to the bonfire together. I didn't see my friends with Jade's girlfriends so I went off looking for them."

"Why didn't you stay with Jade for the rest of the night?" Claire asked.

AJ gave a shrug. "I guess I felt uncomfortable. No one likes being rejected."

"From the sound of it, Jade didn't reject you. She said she'd like to see you again after she broke up with her boyfriend," Claire pointed out.

"Well, who knows if she said that so as not to be hurtful. Maybe she didn't really mean it at all and was just blowing me off." A quick annoyed expression passed over the man's face. "It doesn't matter now. I'll never know if she meant what she said or not."

Claire's sixth sense pinged. "Why won't you ever know?"

Confusion showed over AJ's face. "Because Jade is ...." He stopped talking.

"Jade is what?" Claire asked.

AJ's cheeks reddened. "She's been missing for a while. I ... I thought the chances were...." He let his voice trail off. "I don't know. I guess I didn't think...."

"You think Jade is dead?"

AJ cleared his throat. "It's likely, isn't it? Do you think she could still be alive?"

Although Claire didn't think the young woman

was still alive, she didn't want to reveal her thoughts to AJ. "It's possible, isn't it?"

"I guess it is. I guess I'm a pessimist. I thought law enforcement was treating it like a homicide." AJ picked up his glass and took a long swallow.

Claire watched the man's face. "Why did you think that? Did an officer suggest that?"

"Um. I don't remember. Maybe? I had that impression, but I don't specifically know why. People were talking about it. I must have picked up the idea from other people."

"What kind of a car do you drive?" Claire asked.

AJ told her the make and model.

"Kind of an expensive vehicle for a college student."

"It was a gift."

"What color is it?"

"Red."

"Someone at a convenience store in Hadwen reported a red car like yours at the gas pumps on the night Jade went missing." Claire stared at the young man.

AJ seemed to weighing his options. "I was there getting gas."

"Jade was with you?"

"We went for a ride," AJ admitted. "I stopped for gas, then we went back to the bonfire like I said."

"Why did you leave out the part about going for a ride together?" Claire asked.

"Look. I didn't do anything to Jade. I thought people wouldn't believe me if I said we drove around." AJ ran his hand over his hair.

"I see." Claire changed the subject to throw AJ off. "What are you studying?"

"What?" AJ looked blank for a few moments. "I'm studying business."

"What do you plan to do after graduation?"

"I'm going to join my father's company." AJ appeared a little unsettled by the sudden change of topic.

"What business is your father in?" Claire asked.

"Real estate development."

"Is it a large company?"

"Yes, it is."

"What will your role be?"

"It hasn't been finalized yet. I still have my senior year to complete." AJ fiddled with the end of his fork.

"It sounds like an exciting opportunity." Claire smiled.

"It is." AJ nodded. "It's expected that we'll join the firm when our schooling is completed."

"You have a brother?"

AJ seemed surprised that Claire knew some things about him. "Yes. He's older. He's already been working with our father for a couple of years."

"Your brother is getting married soon, isn't he?"

"Yes, he is."

"I believe my friend, Nicole, has the contract for the desserts for the wedding," Claire said warmly.

"Does she?"

"I work with Nicole on a part time basis. I'll be helping out with the sweets."

"That's a coincidence." AJ shifted his position on the chair again.

Claire looked at the young man's hands. "What happened to your hands? They look pretty scratched up."

"Oh." AJ glanced down and then put his hands in his lap. "I was running. I run on the trails around the college. I'm on the cross-country team. I wasn't paying attention. I fell and went flying and I slid right into a thorn bush. Stupid." He shrugged. "I'll be more careful in the future. I could have broken something and that would have ended my training for the season."

"It was just your hands that got scraped up? I don't see anything on your face."

"I was lucky. My face didn't get scratched."

"What about your arms? Did you injure them?" Claire couldn't see the skin on AJ's arms because of the long-sleeved shirt he was wearing.

"Some. My hands took the brunt of it." AJ took a look at his fancy watch. "I'm sorry, but I need to get going. Is there anything else?"

"No, thanks. I'm all set." Claire leaned back against her seat. "For now."

13

"The guy could be telling the truth," Ian said. "Maybe he *did* walk Jade back to the bonfire."

Claire, Ian, Bear, and Lady strolled over the white sand of the Bayside town beach. When the leashes were removed, the two Corgis took off towards the waves taking turns chasing each other.

High cloud cover hid the sun and made the late afternoon feel chillier than the thermometer reported it to be. Claire wanted to visit the place where Jade had spent a lot of time so she asked Ian to accompany her to the beach. She was feeling glum and the slate gray sky mirrored her mood.

"Maybe he *was* telling the truth." Claire kicked off her shoes and wiggled her toes under the sand. "I had odd sensations when I talked to AJ, but as usual, I can't sort them out. I didn't care for his over-confidence, but maybe it was just me turning my feelings of insecurity from childhood into dislike for him." Claire had grown up poor, she and her loving mother always just a paycheck away from losing their home.

"You can talk to Jade's friends to see if any of them recall seeing AJ walking back to the park with Jade," Ian said. "There had to be someone who saw them returning to the bonfire. I'll pass the information on to my detective friend."

The tide was high and the waves crashed against the sand causing the dogs to jump and bark and run.

"Jade lived three blocks from here, in that direction." Claire pointed. "The family came here all the time, in every season, to swim in the summer, walk the beach, play catch, visit the pier."

Ian stopped and looked out at the rough sea. "Her mother told you this was her daughter's favorite place. Does Mrs. Lyons still come here? Does it give her solace or does it make things worse by reminding her that Jade is missing?"

"She told me it's comforting to be here. It makes her feel close to her daughter." Claire sank down to sit in the sand and Ian did the same.

"What happened?" Claire asked. "How did Jade disappear from a crowded park? She was at the bonfire having a good time and then an hour later, no one knows where she is."

Ian frowned. "*Someone* knows where she is."

Claire picked up a handful of sand and let the grains fall slowly through her fingers. "We just have to find the person who knows."

Bear and Lady raced from the edge of the water, up over the sand, and then trotted around Claire and Ian, barking.

"Hush, you two," Claire told them. "You're too loud."

The dogs usually obeyed their owner, but this time, they kept running and pushing at Claire with their noses.

"The beach makes them nuts," Ian smiled.

"Bear. Lady. Stop." Claire used a firm voice. "No barking."

The dogs sat down at the same time and stared at the young woman.

"Good, dogs. Go play." She gestured down the beach. "Go ahead."

The Corgis hesitated, and then reluctantly walked away, sniffing intently at the sand as they went.

"AJ Phelps's brother is getting married soon. That's the wedding we're doing the desserts for," Claire told her boyfriend.

Ian's eyes widened. "That's an odd coincidence."

"Isn't it?" Claire said. "Maybe I can snoop around the place while we're catering the wedding."

Ian shook his head. "I don't think you'll manage that. There will be hundreds of guests. Someone will spot you looking around and report you to Mr. and Mrs. Phelps who will then fire you."

Claire chuckled. "It will be too late to fire us. They will have already paid us."

"Then you'll end up in jail," Ian said.

"For what? Looking at things?"

"Attempted robbery."

"Yes, attempted robbery of information."

Ian said, "In all seriousness, these people will have security on the premises. No way you'll be able to go anywhere except the kitchen and the wedding tents. You won't be able to find out anything."

"I feel like I might be able to," Claire said in a whisper.

"*Feel* as in a paranormal thing or a regular-person thing?" Ian had a worried look on his face.

"I don't think it's a regular-person feeling."

Ian gave Claire a sideways glance and took her

hand. "Just be very careful. The person responsible for Jade's disappearance could be at that wedding. Keep your eyes open. Stay on your toes. I'll tell Nicole to do the same. And call me if anything seems off ... anything at all."

Claire squeezed Ian's hand and leaned her shoulder against his. "I will."

"Maybe I should go along with you to the wedding. I can pretend to be your assistant."

"Sorry," Claire smiled. "The contract says only three of us can be working that afternoon and evening. It's Nicole, me, and Robby."

"Maybe I'll take Robby's place so I can protect you."

"Then you'd have to learn to decorate cakes before we go. You don't have enough time."

"You doubt my abilities?" Ian asked in mock offense.

Claire stood up to go. "Yup."

CLAIRE, Ian, Nicole, and Ryan sat on the Back Bay restaurant's patio next to the glowing pyramid-shaped heaters that warmed the air. The clouds had cleared away since Claire and Ian left the beach and the stars twinkled against the inky sky. The couples chatted, people-watched, and sipped drinks while waiting for their dinners to arrive.

"The Phelps family hosted a big charity event not long ago to raise money for the hospital," Ryan told the group. "It was very successful. They have a lot of important connections, not only in Boston, but around the world. Donors with very deep pockets. I met the family briefly at the event, including AJ. If their son is involved in any way with this young woman's disappearance, it will be a very black mark against the family."

"Aren't people like the Phelps family able to make their troubles go away?" Nicole lifted her wine glass to her lips and looked to Ian for his opinion.

"With some things," Ian said. "But not with murder."

Ryan looked at the detective with a look of surprise. "Murder? Is that what law enforcement thinks now? The young woman has been murdered?"

"If missing people aren't located in the first couple of days, it usually means there won't be a happy ending," Claire explained.

"I didn't realize." A sad look washed over Ryan's

face. "That's terrible. I hope AJ didn't have anything to do with it."

The server who was waiting on the foursome approached the table. "When I walked by a minute ago, I heard you talking about AJ Phelps and that missing girl."

Claire's heart began to pound.

"One of the waitresses here dated AJ last year. Would you like to speak with her? I think she'd have some interesting things to tell you."

Claire spoke up. "Yes, I would, if she doesn't mind. I'm helping the family look into the disappearance."

"Her name is Audra. She went to Whittemore for three years, but had to take this year off to work. She's sitting over there in the red dress. She's not working tonight, just stopped by for a drink. I'll go ask her if you can talk to her for a little bit."

The waitress walked away, stopped at Audra's table, leaned down to speak to her, then looked over to Claire and waved at her to come over.

When Claire went to the young woman's table, she introduced herself.

Audra gestured to the stool on the other side of the high-top table. "I hear you're interested in AJ Phelps." The woman's words slurred together and

Claire wondered how long she'd been sitting there. Audra had white-blond hair that reached way down her back, courtesy of extensions. Her makeup was heavy, but artfully done and she wore black heels and a body-hugging, deep red dress.

Claire explained, "I'm talking to people who know Jade Lyons, trying to help the family find some information. I spoke with AJ yesterday."

"I went to Whittemore and I knew who Jade was, but I don't think we ever spoke." Audra took a swallow from her mixed drink. "Did AJ date her?"

"He didn't date her. He talked to her at a bonfire across the road from Whittemore," Claire said.

"That was the night when Jade went missing, right?" Audra asked.

"Yes."

"Do you think AJ had something to do with it?" When Audra lifted her blue eyes, they held a look of suspicion.

"Why do you ask that?"

"I don't trust AJ. He goes from one woman to the next, sometimes running around with two at the same time. He's careful though. He doesn't date two women from the college because they'd find out. He might date an undergrad and a woman from a nearby town. Less chance of them discovering one another."

"Did he do this when he was dating you?" Claire asked,

"He sure did. Busy, isn't he? I don't know where he gets the energy." Audra took another sip. "Although, AJ doesn't need to work to get through college so he has more time for extracurricular activities than some of us do." The young woman made eye contact with Claire. "So did he have something to do with the girl going missing?"

"Do you think he could do something like that?" Claire asked. "Cause someone to go missing?"

"I don't think AJ has any empathy. He only cares about his own wants and needs. Do I think he could do something wrong? Yes, I do. I think AJ is lacking in the basic humanity that would stop someone else from doing something bad."

The woman's words sent a shudder over Claire and she recalled AJ telling her that Jade had rejected him by wanting to leave his apartment and return to the bonfire. Could that feeling of rejection make him lash out at Jade. "Did AJ ever hit you?"

Audra sat straight. "No way. He knew better than to do that."

"Did he treat you in a bad way?"

Audra smiled sadly. "There was never any overt mistreatment. It was all subtle. Dating other people while we were together, acting like I was wrong to question him, him being drunk a lot, being high a lot, and being defensive when I called him out on it."

"Does AJ have a drinking or a drug problem?" Claire asked.

"I don't know. He'd deny it even if it was true." Audra sighed. "I don't know if he's addicted or might be an alcoholic. I don't know the medical definition of those things. But he drinks a ton and takes drugs." She shook her head slowly. "Have you met his pal?"

"What pal?" Claire's forehead furrowed in thought.

"The drug dealer. He's a fine example of a human being." Audra rolled her eyes. "He's a creep. AJ was always buying from the guy. I'm sure he still is."

Claire's throat tightened. "What's the pal's name?"

Audra leaned forward and spoke in a soft voice. "Badger."

14

"Badger?" Claire asked, her heart thumping. She remembered the convenience store clerk in the small town of Hadwen mentioning a man called Badger being with AJ Phelps the night Jade disappeared.

"Yes, the name is as stupid as he is." Audra ran her hand through her hair extension.

"He's a drug dealer?"

"Yes, and he's as mean as he is stupid," Audra said. "I don't think that guy has a brain in his head. He's like a robot. I drove with AJ once to meet him. Badger was beating up a guy behind a convenience store in Hadwen. He had a knife. I pulled out my phone to call the police and AJ freaked. He batted the phone from my hand. He told me never to call the police on this guy. I told AJ to turn the car around and take me back to campus. I wasn't getting involved with a monster like that. We yelled at each other all the way back."

"So you never actually met this Badger person?" Claire asked.

"And I never will," Audra said.

"Did AJ still buy from the guy?"

"He did, just not with me in the car. I don't ever want to be within one hundred miles of that poor excuse for a human." Audra drained her cocktail. Her eyes had taken on a glassy look while she'd been talking with Claire.

"Are you meeting someone tonight?"

Audra looked confused for a moment. "Oh, yeah. My boyfriend."

"What were you studying at Whittemore?"

A smile crept over the woman's mouth. "Nursing. They have an excellent program. I'm going to finish my final year when I return next year."

"Do you see AJ anymore? Do you run into him at all?" Claire asked.

"I haven't seen him for quite a while," Audra said. "I do occasionally see the missing girl's boyfriend. His first name is Kyle. He comes in here for lunch or dinner sometimes. He works here in the city."

"You know Kyle?"

"I don't really know him. I've waited on him a bunch. Somebody who works here told us the missing woman is Kyle's girlfriend." Audra shuddered. "It shocked me, really shocked me."

"Has Kyle come into the restaurant since Jade went missing?"

"No. At least I haven't seen him," Audra said.

"Does Kyle come in alone?"

"Sometimes. Other times, he comes in with a couple of guys." Audra looked across the patio to the door to the restaurant and lifted her index finger in a gesture to wait. "My boyfriend's here." She collected her phone and her wallet. "If you want to talk more, I'm usually working here in the evenings on Tuesdays, Wednesdays, and Thursdays. Or call the restaurant and ask about my schedule."

Claire thanked the young woman for speaking with her.

Audra let out a long breath. "I can't get Jade out of my mind. What was she? Twenty-one? I'm the same age." Shaking her head, she said, "Whatever happened to her could happen to me." Audra clenched her hand around her phone. "Sometimes I think I'm crazy for obsessing over this."

Claire nodded understandingly. "The idea of Jade being missing is upsetting to you. It's upsetting to people who didn't even know Jade at all. Her disappearance makes people feel very vulnerable."

"I guess." Audra stood up and leaned over the table to shake Claire's hand. "Come by again if you want. We can talk."

Feeling shaky and anxious, Claire got up to return to her friends.

Ian stood when Claire approached her chair and he noticed her gait was slightly unstable. "Are you okay?"

"I'm fine." Why did what Claire heard from Audra cause her legs to go weak? Badger, the mean drug dealer. AJ interacting with a drug dealer. AJ claiming that he walked Jade back to the bonfire. Did anyone see them returning to the fire? Who is keeping things hidden? Who is lying? Who is telling the truth?

Words and images swirled so rapidly in Claire's brain that she became slightly dizzy and was grateful for Ian's strong, warm hand on the small of her back.

CLAIRE HAD BEEN DREADING the early morning meeting in the chocolate shop. She hadn't seen Mrs. Lyons for a few days and even though she didn't like to admit it, she hadn't missed the smothering heaviness of the woman's grief pressing against her.

Bonnie Lyons looked pale and thin and her hair hung down dull and lifeless. Claire guessed she hadn't been eating much or sleeping and the lack of food and rest was catching up with her and showing on her face.

"How's your older daughter doing?" Claire asked.

A joyless smile tugged at the corners of Bonnie's lips. "Jeena's holding up better than I am. Or maybe she hides it better than I do. She's busy back at work and I think that's a helpful distraction for her. Did you go to the beach?"

Claire nodded. "We walked my dogs there. I looked around. It's a beautiful spot."

"Jade and I loved it there." Bonnie looked out of the shop's window.

The past tense, Claire noted. Bonnie used the past tense when she mentioned Jade.

"Who have you been able to talk to?" Bonnie held the mug of hot coffee between her hands.

Claire listed the people she'd spoken with and provided some details from the conversations.

"Did anything someone say point to a place Jade might be?" Bonnie asked with the tiniest trace of hope in her voice.

"No, nothing," Claire said. "I want to follow up with the three men I've spoken with already. I feel there's more there to draw out."

Bonnie crossed her arms on the table. "Do any of them seem guilty?"

Even if Claire had a strong feeling that someone she'd spoken with was the one responsible for Jade's disappearance, she wouldn't tell Bonnie unless she had some hard evidence to go on. She worried Bonnie would rush off determined to exact revenge and end up confronting the wrong person.

"Almost every person I've talked with could be thought of as having motive," Claire said. "But having a motive isn't the same as being guilty of hurting someone."

Bonnie flinched at the words *hurting someone.* "You're right. We have to be sure."

"Have you spoken with the police?"

With a weak nod, Bonnie said, "They're always very nice to me, but I can feel their pity. They don't think I'm able to help, but who else involved in searching for my daughter has a motive similar to mine? My love for my daughter is my motivation to find her. No one else has that ... no one else will go to the ends of the earth for my Jade."

Something Bonnie said caused a thought to float by in Claire's brain, but it was foggy and unformed and she couldn't grasp it. But she knew it was important.

"Do the police have any leads about the things they found that belonged to Jade? Her phone, fleece jacket, and driver's license?" Claire questioned.

"Not really. They don't think Jade was the one who piled her things neatly in that lot," Bonnie said. "They think she was with someone and that person ended up placing her belongings there. *Why* it was done is another question without an answer."

"Did the person think by neatly piling the things that we'd all think Jade committed suicide?" Claire asked. "Did the person think that if we believed Jade killed herself, then he'd be safe from an investigation? The focus would shift and he wouldn't be found out?"

"It's possible." Bonnie's hand shook as she lifted her mug. "Jade did not kill herself."

"I know," Claire told her.

"We've organized ten different searches of several

areas," Bonnie said. "I've talked to Jade's friends and I've gone through her emails, her texts. The police did the same. We get nowhere, we find nothing."

"There is still a lot to do," Claire used a reassuring tone. "I talked to AJ Phelps, but I need to speak with him again. He told me he and Jade went back to the bonfire after leaving it for a little while. The convenience store clerk told us Jade was waiting inside while AJ filled his gas tank. We need to know if Jade was in AJ's car when he returned to campus."

"Did you ask AJ about that drug dealer?" Bonnie asked.

"No. I'll bring that up next time we meet. I'd already caught him in a lie and I didn't want to scare him off," Claire said.

"Try to talk to him again soon," Bonnie said. "Winter's coming. We're running out of time."

15

"Why did you want to come back here?" Nicole asked as she and Claire and the Corgis left the car and walked onto the Bayside town beach.

The day was unusually warm with the sun shining in a bright blue sky, and a number of people sat in chairs while others rested on blankets soaking up the sun on what was surely the last beach day of the year. A few brave people were even body-surfing in the chilly waves.

"I don't know why. Since I was here with Ian, something's been itching at me to come back." Claire let the dogs off the leashes and they raced off to meet and sniff another dog.

"It's a great day for the beach so it's fine with

me." Nicole spread a blanket and the young women sat down. "A chance to get a little more sun before the snow flies in a month or two." With a sigh, she asked, "Where does the time go? The summer was over in a flash. It's October already."

"Jade loved this beach," Claire said as she looked out over the blue sea.

"I can see why. It's a beautiful spot. The family was lucky to live so close by," Nicole said.

"Bonnie Lyons told me she felt badly when Jade had to live at home this semester. Money was always tight and when their roof had to be replaced unexpectedly, there went the college room and board money. Bonnie said Jade claimed she didn't mind living at home and was happy to spend more time with her mom, and that it gave her more time to come down to the beach," Claire said. "Jade sounds like a good person."

"We haven't heard a single bad thing about her," Nicole agreed. "Everyone has had good things to say." Eyeing her friend, she asked, "Do you have any *feelings* about any of the people we've talked to? Does anyone stand out on your paranormal radar?"

Claire smiled at Nicole's description of her skill. "I've had odd sensations with almost everyone we've talked with, but nothing really stands out. AJ is suspicious. Badger was at that convenience store when Jade was there. Blake Rhodes cheated on Jade when they dated and recently got in touch with her. Why did he? Kyle Vallins didn't seem that upset about the situation, but he had begun distancing himself from Jade anticipating a breakup. Maybe none of these people had anything to do with Jade's disappearance. It could have been random. Jade might have been walking back to campus and someone snatched her."

"The police still don't have any leads?" Nicole asked.

"Ian says no, but the investigators up here might not be sharing everything with him."

"Look at those nutty dogs," Nicole said with a chuckle. "They're digging down to the center of the earth."

Claire looked to the left to see Bear and Lady digging together in the sand. She whistled to them, but they ignored her. Pushing herself up from the blanket, she headed to where they were making the hole. "I don't want them digging like that. Someone will come by later and twist an ankle."

When she called to the dogs, Lady lifted her head, but kept right on pawing the sand. Claire clapped her hands and spoke their names in a firm voice. "No, no."

With reluctant looks, the dogs stopped digging and barked at Claire.

"Hush now. Come on. We'll get kicked off the beach." When Claire turned around to go back to the blanket, a young woman stood nearby admiring the Corgis.

"What beautiful dogs." The woman had long brown hair pulled back in a ponytail and big blue eyes. She wore a tank top and shorts and carried her flip-flops in one hand.

When Bear and Lady spotted her, they trotted over to the brunette to receive some petting.

Claire said, "They're good dogs, but they're excited to be here and they're having a hard time listening to me this afternoon. That one's Bear and the other one is Lady."

The young woman chuckled as Bear licked her hand. "A bit of selective hearing? Only hearing what they want to hear today?"

"That's right."

"Are you visiting?" the young woman asked. "I don't remember seeing the dogs here before."

"We live in Boston. The weather is so great today, we decided to come up. Do you live nearby?"

Nicole walked over and introduced herself, and then joked. "No one would ever talk to us if we didn't have these two dogs around."

"It's true. I'm Claire by the way."

"Maggie. I live a few blocks away. I grew up in town."

Claire's head buzzed.

"Do you know Jade Lyons?" Nicole asked.

Bear and Lady whined softly.

Maggie's face took on a pained expression. "Yes." The young woman swallowed. "Jade and I were friends since we were little."

"Do you go to the same college?" Nicole questioned.

"No." Maggie shook her head. "I was never good at school. College isn't for me."

"What do you do?" Claire asked.

"I went to school for hairdressing. I've been saving since I was a little kid. I just opened my own shop on Main Street," Maggie told them. "It's small, but it's a beginning."

Nicole and Claire offered their congratulations.

"Did you still see Jade? Did you still have time to see each other, what with her in college and you starting your own business?" Nicole asked.

"We kept in touch. We'd get together once in a

while, have dinner, come to the beach. She was living at home this semester so we got together a few times. Jade brought flowers over to my shop to wish me well."

Claire smiled. "Jade sounds like a nice person."

"She was always nice to me." A soft smile lifted the corners of Maggie's lips. "Some of the girls didn't bother with me because I wasn't in the top classes with them, but not Jade. She always treated me as an equal. She'd help me with math or writing a report. Jade always said being smart in school didn't decide a person's success. It was about knowing what you wanted and working hard to get it. She made me feel good." Maggie's face became serious. "You know what happened, right?"

"Jade is missing," Nicole said.

Maggie nodded. "It doesn't make sense. Jade is a great person. She's nice to everyone. She wants to be a physical therapist so she can help people. How can she be missing? What could have happened?"

Bear rubbed his head against Maggie's leg.

"When was the last time you saw Jade?" Claire asked.

"The day she brought me the flowers."

"When was that?" Claire questioned.

"The day before she disappeared." Maggie's eyes

had misted over. "Jade came to the shop with the flowers. She asked if I had time to go for a walk on the beach. I didn't. I had a million things to do. I was opening in two days. I should have gone with her. I should have left the shop for a while and gone for the walk." Maggie brushed at her eyes. "What if I never see her again?"

Claire's heart clenched. "I'm sure Jade understood. You had to get the shop ready."

"Jade said she'd try to come back to help me out," Maggie said shaking her head. "She didn't get the chance."

"Do you know Cori Ball?" Nicole asked.

"Cori grew up in town. She was Jade's roommate at Whittemore ... until this year."

"Were you and Cori friends?" Claire asked.

"Not really. Friendly, but not friends. Cori could be kind of snooty with me."

"Jade got along with her?"

"Yeah, she did. Jade told me Cori had changed though. She could be very moody. Jade said whenever a guy talked to her, Cori would get all jealous. She wasn't that easy to live with, I guess."

"Did Jade ever talk about trouble with Cori?" Nicole asked.

"Not really trouble. More like she wished Cori would be more easy-going."

"You must know Kyle Vallins?" Claire asked.

"Sure. He's lived in town since he was little. Kyle is Jade's boyfriend."

"Do you know him well?"

"Pretty well. Some of us would hang out together. He liked to talk to me. People tell me I'm a good listener."

"Did the two of you date?"

"Us? No. Never. It wasn't like that. Kyle always liked Jade. Even in elementary school. He and I were always friends."

"Have you seen Kyle lately?" Claire asked.

"He came by a couple of days after Jade went missing," Maggie said. "I was working late at the shop, cleaning up, finishing some painting I didn't get to. He'd had too much to drink." The young woman took in a long breath. "He was crying, sobbing really. He was so upset about Jade. I was upset, too. We both cried together."

Bear let out a low growl and Claire looked down at him.

"What did Kyle say when he was with you at the shop?" Nicole asked.

Maggie's forehead creased. "He went on and on

asking why did this happen? Why did he have to lose Jade? Things like that. He was a real mess. He brought a six pack into the shop, but he was already drunk. It seemed like he didn't hear a word I was saying to him. He just sobbed and sobbed. It was heartbreaking. I started drinking with him. I was already upset about Jade before Kyle came to the door. I was thinking how Jade would never see my place all finished. Jade always encouraged me, said I'd make a great businessperson. I would have liked her to see what was happening for me."

"Do you think you won't see Jade again?" Claire asked gently.

"I'd love to be wrong, but she's been gone a week now." Maggie's lip quivered. "I don't have much hope." The young woman shifted her gaze out to the water. "You know, I've been dreaming about her. She's under water, in the ocean. She can't find her way to the top. She's panicking. Then I wake up in a cold sweat. Why do I always dream she's drowning in the ocean?"

The image of Jade under the water unable to surface made Claire's palms go clammy and her heart pound.

Bear barked causing Claire to startle.

"From what I've heard, Jade loved the beach and

the sea," Claire said, trying to keep her voice even and calm. "You associate Jade with the ocean. Somehow, she's gone missing. Jade, the ocean, and the sense of distress mix together in your mind when you're dreaming."

"It makes sense," Maggie said. "I'd better get back. I always have a lot to do."

The women said goodbye and Maggie bent to pat the Corgis before heading back to the road.

Claire turned and stared at the ocean before moving her gaze to the pier. "Why do I think that running into Maggie was a fortunate encounter?"

Nicole narrowed her eyes. "Because it was."

16

The late afternoon sky was slate gray and heavy with rain threatening to fall at any moment. Claire, Nicole, and Robby had just arrived after closing the chocolate shop for the day and they stepped out of the car wearing rain slickers and boots.

"Of course, it couldn't be sunny and warm like the other day when we were here." Nicole closed the buttons on her raincoat.

"Let's hope we can find something that will help the case." Robby adjusted his baseball cap as he looked over to the pier. "Should we wait for Mrs. Lyons or should we go look around?"

"Let's wait," Claire said.

After meeting Maggie Burns on the beach yesterday, Claire called Bonnie Lyons to talk about Jade.

"I feel the town beach could hold a clue," Claire had told Bonnie. "I don't know why, but I'm drawn there. I think we should take a closer look around the pier."

The phone had been silent for so long that Claire thought the call had dropped, but then Bonnie made a sniffing sound and her voice was heavy when she said, "The beach has been on my mind, too. It's not far from Whittemore or the convenience store where Jade was last seen. At night ... in the fall ... there wouldn't be many people around. It would be easy to drive up and...."

The woman didn't need to finish the sentence for Claire to know what she meant. It wouldn't be hard to dump a body there.

"I'm going to the pier to look around," Claire had said.

"I'm going with you," Bonnie said, and despite Claire's concerns that it might be best for the woman not to be with them should they find something about Jade or maybe, find her body, Bonnie wasn't having any of it. "I'm not going to sit here at home twiddling my fingers. I'm going along. I'm going to search for my daughter."

With a sigh, Claire had reluctantly agreed and they made arrangements to meet at the beach the next afternoon.

Bonnie Lyons arrived wearing a knitted hat pulled down over her head, a yellow slicker, and work boots. Her face was tight as she shoved her hands into her pockets.

"I thought we could walk the beach first," Claire suggested, so the group spread out along the sand and began to move down the beach to the jetty.

"Kyle Vallins grew up in Bayside," Claire said to Bonnie who was walking along beside her. "Does he come to the beach much? Does he like the water?"

Bonnie's voice was hoarse. "He keeps kayaks by the pier on the harbor side. He can sail. He worked a few summers on the lobster boat tours taking guests out to see the process of lobstering. Kyle and Jade liked coming down to swim and boogie board."

The breeze kicked up and blew some sand into their faces.

"Why are you asking about Kyle and the beach?" Bonnie looked sideways at Claire.

"I'm trying to find out who might know things about the area." Claire didn't want to admit that Kyle was on her suspect list. "What about Jade's former boyfriend, Blake? Did he come to this beach?"

Bonnie said, "Blake didn't grow up here. He wasn't familiar with the town. He and Jade came down to swim a couple of times. Jade told me he wasn't a very good swimmer."

"Do you know AJ Phelps?" Claire asked.

"I know who the family is. We don't exactly move in the same social circles. They live in Boston, but they also have a house on the hill overlooking the harbor. A mansion, actually. I've never met any of the Phelps family. They keep boats in the harbor, a speedboat, a sailboat ... I think there's a cabin cruiser, too. The whole family seems to know their way around boats. I've seen them heading in and out of the harbor." Bonnie wiped some moisture from her cheeks. A heavy mist and fog was in the air which decreased the group's visibility to a few feet in front of them. "Why are you asking about the Phelps family?"

Claire didn't want to give Bonnie a lot of details. "AJ knew Jade at school. He's a senior at Whittemore, too."

"The three young men ... are they suspects?" Bonnie's tone was hard. "Kyle, too?"

"Everyone is a suspect in my eyes," Claire sighed. "I don't have anything on the young men. I'm just covering bases and gathering information."

Bonnie bent and picked something up from the sand and after checking it, she tossed it back down. "I thought it might be a ring. Let's move closer to the tide line."

The tide was high and huge waves crashed against the shore sending a cool mist into the air. Claire's long hair was damp and dripping.

"You think Jade went into the water?" Bonnie asked softly.

Claire looked the woman in the eye. "I don't know. If she did, she didn't go voluntarily. I don't have any strong reasons to be down here looking around. I don't have any reasons to point the finger at one particular person. It's just ... I don't know. I didn't think it would hurt to look around even though I have no idea what I expect to find."

"I have the same feelings," Bonnie admitted as she wiped at her eye. "Every time I come down here, I feel Jade. It's probably because we spent so much time here, I remember all of our happy times. Being on this beach makes me feel close to her."

The group approached the jetty.

"Do you want to walk out on it?" Robby had to raise his voice over the crashing waves and the wind that had picked up.

Claire watched a few waves break over the far

end of the jetty. "I think it's too dangerous to go out there."

Bonnie moved closer to the jetty and hunched over looking at the nooks and crannies in the piled up rocks. The others did the same thing, but without climbing up on the jetty.

Nicole sidled up to Claire. "This search freaks me out. I'm a nervous wreck. I want to find something that will help, but I *do not* want to find a body. Every time I think I see something, my heart stops. I don't know how Bonnie can handle this."

The fog rolled in and obscured the pier from view. It was time to head in that direction.

When the four of them got closer, Claire could make out the seaweed and old fishing nets wrapped up together and tucked around the base of the pier's support columns. Some pieces of driftwood, an old, broken-up lobster trap, and various shells could be seen when the waves rolled in and out. Rain started and mixed with the fog and the spray off the ocean.

Robby wore boots up to his knees. "I'll walk under the pier and check around the columns and pilings." He had to raise his voice to be heard.

As he headed into the cold water, Claire and Bonnie moved to the far side to begin their search beneath the tall pier. Nicole walked slowly along the water's edge, but the waves hit her in the legs and drenched her so she gave up trying to stay dry and ventured out under the middle of the structure.

The pull of the tide was strong and the searchers had to hold onto the columns when a particularly large wave encircled their legs.

When the waves retreated before crashing forward again, they bent over and scanned the ground for anything belonging to Jade, a barrette, a piece of clothing, a piece of jewelry that may have wedged itself into the sand.

Robby tugged at some of the nets so he could examine them for anything that might indicate Jade had been nearby and when Nicole saw what he was doing, she strode through the waves to go help him.

The rain fell harder, but it didn't matter since each person was soaked to the bone already.

When the wet and cold became too much causing Claire to shake and shiver, she called to the others and gestured for the beach.

"Why don't we take a walk on the pier and have a look around from up there," she suggested.

Bonnie looked out from under the pier with an expression of defeat and disappointment.

Nicole put her hand on the woman's arm and gently nudged her out from under.

On top of the pier, the wind and rain buffeted them and made their movements unsteady.

"Where did this come from?" Robby almost yelled to be heard over what seemed like near gale-force winds and he had to lean into the blowing air to move forward.

When they reached the end, the four watched the water below heaving and churning, and Claire was sure that if anything of Jade's had gone into the ocean, it must be across the Atlantic by now.

She scanned the harbor to her right. The boats rose and fell with the waves and yanked on the ropes that tethered them. Claire didn't think they were wrong to come there, but where were the clues? Where was Jade?

With a sinking heart, Claire led the way down the length of the pier and back to the beach where they'd started.

"I'm sorry we didn't find anything." Claire wrapped Bonnie in a hug.

"We tried. It's okay." Strands of her hair pasted to her cheeks, Bonnie wiped at her wet face with her wet hand. "We'll figure it out. We can't give up." She glanced back at the angry ocean. Her bottom lip quivered and she tried to collect herself, but the wind and the rain and the cold had beaten her down.

Bonnie hunched over, buried her face in her hands, and sobbed.

17

"You and Nicole need a night off from all of this sadness." Robby placed bowls of corn chowder and plates with a focaccia sandwich of grilled vegetables, sundried tomatoes, hummus, and goat cheese on the placemats. A small round table decorated with lit candles sat in front of a big window with a view of the Boston skyline, and Claire, Nicole, and Robby crowded around it.

"I didn't know you could cook." Nicole dabbed at her lips with her napkin. "Yum."

"I'm a man of many talents." Robby passed around a plate of sweet potato fries.

After leaving the beach, the wet and miserable group returned to their homes for hot showers and a change of clothes and then Claire and Nicole met up at Robby's studio apartment for dinner.

"Your place is gorgeous," Claire said as she lifted her soup spoon. "I love it."

Robby had added his own touches to the small apartment making it seem like something out of a magazine. With the landlord's blessing, he'd added crystal chandeliers, painted the walls creamy white, and decorated the space with beautiful furniture he'd picked up at flea markets or from the city sidewalks left out by people giving the items away.

"You have a real eye for decorating," Claire told him. "I need you to redo my place."

"If the price is right." Robby winked. "So, Clairvoyant Claire, what do your senses tell you about this case?"

Nicole scowled. "I thought tonight was a reprieve from the disappearance of Jade Lyons."

"Tonight is a reprieve from *active* investigation," Robby corrected. "I never said we weren't going to discuss it." The young man poured red wine into each of the glasses. "I think discussion in a relaxing setting might enhance the brain's ability to reason and think. So? Are your senses telling you anything?"

Claire frowned. "They seem to have deserted me

in my time of need."

"I don't think that's it," Robby said.

Claire and Nicole stared at the young man.

"How do you know anything about *special* skills?" Nicole questioned, her eyes wide.

"I don't know specifically about Claire's clairvoyance, but I know when I'm stressed for an audition or a show, my mind kind of goes blank. Everything I've learned in school, my preparation, and all my experience seem to fade away, leaving me feeling insecure and unable to perform to my ability."

Claire leaned forward. "How do you break out of it? How do you get your skills to kick in?"

"By doing something relaxing like taking a walk, baking, reading a good book, and using self-talk. I remind myself that I'm talented and capable and well-prepared. I need to cast off negative thoughts. They're unhelpful and wrong and will keep me from doing my best. You need to try it," Robby looked at Claire. "Do you feel tense right now?"

Claire moved her shoulders around. "A little."

"About the case?" Robby asked.

"About how little progress we've made. About all the time we spent in the terrible weather this afternoon and then coming up with nothing." Claire shook her head.

"Okay," Robby said. "Just because we came away empty-handed, that doesn't mean your skills aren't working. You have the idea the beach is important. You feel it. You sense it. Your skill *is* working. You just need to keep looking."

"It makes sense. You're right." Claire gave Robby a warm smile. "How come you're so smart?"

Robby shrugged. "I'm a performer. If I don't have ways to deal with stress, I'll never work."

"Let's talk about the case," Claire sipped from her glass. "Kyle Vallins, AJ Phelps, and Blake Rhodes all had motivation and all had access to Jade."

Nicole said, "But Blake claims he wasn't at the bonfire. He says he stayed in Boston that night."

"How do we know he isn't lying?" Claire asked. "We need to find someone who saw him in the city."

"What about Kyle?" Robby asked. "He told you he was with friends and he didn't see Jade at all. Do you believe him?"

"Again, we'll have to talk to the guys he was supposedly with," Claire said.

"And there's AJ," Nicole said. "He says he was with Jade. They went to his apartment for a while and then they drove around. AJ had to be confronted about driving around, he didn't tell us upfront because he was afraid it would make him seem guilty to be with Jade in a car."

Claire added, "AJ says he walked Jade back to the bonfire and then he went looking for his friends."

"Can anyone corroborate AJ's claim that he was back in the park with Jade after their joy ride?" Robby asked.

"We need to talk to people about that," Claire said. "We should talk to the friends, Cori and Alyssa, again." Rubbing at her forehead, she said, "If AJ brought Jade back to the bonfire, why didn't anyone see her there?"

"I can think of a reason why no one saw her there," Nicole said.

Claire and Robby waited.

"Because AJ never brought her back. He's lying. I bet he left her at that convenience store."

"I bet you're right." Claire stood up. "Anyone want to go for a ride?"

"Where to?" Nicole asked.

"The convenience store," Claire said.

"But we haven't had dessert yet," Robby said. "We'll go the store, but first, we're going to finish this meal. It's part of the necessary relaxation to reduce stress. Have a seat and enjoy the chocolate mousse I made. We'll be done in five minutes."

NICOLE DROVE into the parking lot of the convenience store and pulled into a spot at the rear of the building. When they were getting out, Claire spotted the clerk they spoke with last time, standing behind the building smoking. She took a quick look at them, stubbed out her cigarette, and dashed inside.

"Someone isn't very friendly," Robby observed.

"I guess she doesn't want to talk to us," Claire said.

"Your powers of observation are quite impressive," Robby joked.

"Come on," Nicole said. "She's going to talk to us whether she wants to or not."

Claire followed her friend wondering how Nicole thought they might get Brenda to talk if she didn't want to engage in conversation with them.

When they entered the brightly-lit store, Brenda saw them and started for the backroom.

"Can you spare a few minutes?" Claire asked.

"No," Brenda said in a huff.

"Could you ring this up for me?" Robby held up a box of candy.

"No." Brenda stopped her race for the stock

room. "I don't want to talk. Go away and leave me alone."

"I'll be quick," Claire said. "I promise."

"Your promises don't mean nothing to me." Brenda stood with her hand on her hip in a defensive stance.

"Do you take smoking breaks regularly during your shifts?" Claire asked.

"The management doesn't care. It's okay with them," Brenda said.

"I'm only asking because if you smoke at the same spot as I saw you just now, you can see the back of the parking lot."

"So?" Brenda asked.

"So, you might have seen Jade," Nicole was exasperated. "She might have gotten into a car right as you were going out to smoke that night. Maybe you saw her."

"I don't remember much of the night," Brenda said. "I have some memory issues."

"I'm sorry to hear that," Claire said. "But did you notice Jade at the rear of the store?"

"Did you notice if there was a car there at the time?" Robby asked.

"Did you see Jade out there?" Nicole asked.

"I didn't notice," Brenda said.

"When I was here last time," Claire said, "You told me Jade was in the store texting. That she might have been upset. And then a guy opened the door and asked Jade if she was ready. Did she leave the store with the guy?"

"The girl left the store. I don't know if she left with the guy." Brenda crossed her arms over her chest.

"You mentioned a drug dealer," Nicole started to ask a question.

Brenda's eyes widened in horror. "I never mentioned any such thing. Where'd you get that? I didn't say it."

Claire asked, "Did you smoke that night? Did you go outside?"

"I don't remember."

"Can you think back?" Claire asked. "Can you try to picture Jade? Did she leave the store with the guy who talked to her?"

"She left the store. After that I don't know what happened."

"When you were smoking out back, did you notice anyone or maybe, a car parked away from the others?" Claire questioned.

"I told you. I don't recall."

"Maybe the person Jade texted came to get her."

Claire kept her voice soft. "Did you notice a car near the back of the store?"

Brenda' shoulders crumpled. "There was a car. I don't know who it belonged to. I don't know who got into the driver's seat."

"Did Jade...?"

"She got in on the passenger side."

"Was the guy who came into the shop and talked to Jade the driver of the car?"

"I have no idea," Brenda said. "Like I told you, there weren't many cars around that night."

"What kind of a car did Jade get into?" Nicole asked.

"A van. I remember a van. It was parked at the back corner of the lot. I didn't see who was driving it." Brenda glanced to the front door.

"What color was it?"

"It was a dark color. I couldn't see that good. Dark blue?"

"Did you see Jade with the drug dealer?" Nicole asked.

Brenda's face flushed in anger. "I told you there's no drugs here. I told you I don't know nothing about any dealer. You need to leave. Now."

Claire's mind raced. *A van.*

18

"You've heard about the Whittemore student who has gone missing?" Claire sat at the bar of the expensive South End restaurant with Bob Cooney, a former private investigator who now was known to be employed in a variety of shady dealings. A thin, wiry man in his mid to late fifties with jet black hair, he had a reputation as a guy who knew what was going on in the city. He'd helped Claire a few times, some of which she'd paid handsomely for.

"I don't live under a rock, Rollins." Cooney sipped from his glass of scotch. "Of course I know about the missing woman."

"The young woman's mother asked me to help her look into the disappearance," Claire said.

"Why?"

"Someone told her I have strong intuition."

"And deep pockets," Cooney said.

"She doesn't know that."

"The mother isn't happy with the police work that's being done?" Cooney was dressed in designer slacks and a perfectly pressed shirt. He held court nearly every afternoon at the bar regaling attractive young women with stories about his escapades. Claire was early and the place was fairly empty, but she knew Cooney would dump her as soon as a beautiful well-dressed women arrived for drinks or dinner. She needed to talk fast.

"She *is* happy with the police. But she wants to find her daughter so she's using every resource available."

"She should come talk to me," Cooney said and glanced around the bar for someone more interesting than Claire to talk to.

"*I'm* talking to you," Claire reminded the man. "Do you know anything?"

Cooney held his glass. "I know a lot of things."

Claire clarified. "Do you know anything about this case?"

"Negative." Cooney turned on his stool to face Claire.

"Then I guess our conversation is over." Claire reached for her purse and was about to get up.

"Can't you tell when someone is fooling around?" Cooney said. "No need to rush off."

"You do know something?"

"I know a lot about a lot of things," Cooney said.

Claire sighed. "Why do we always have to talk in riddles? Can't you just tell me what you know and we can be done?"

Cooney tilted his head to the side. "If I did that, then you wouldn't develop any investigative skills at all. I ask questions that make you think. It improves your cognition." The man tapped his temple with his index finger.

"Maybe you should teach at a university," Claire deadpanned.

"Nah. My life is perfect the way it is." Cooney adjusted his cufflink.

Claire decided to play the game. "I'm assuming Jade is dead."

"I'd bet money you are probably correct."

"Did someone kill her?"

Cooney made a face. "Really, Rollins? What do you think happened to her? She jetted off to Europe for a few weeks with some rock star?"

Claire became impatient. "Do you know who killed her?"

"No, I don't." Cooney eyed Claire. "But I bet you do."

With her eyes narrowed and her lips tight, Claire asked herself why it was like this every time she talked to Cooney. "How would you know that?"

"I hear things. I understand you've been talking to a lot of people."

"I've talked to a good number."

"Keep doing what you're doing," Cooney said and eyed a tall blonde in a tight dress who had just entered the bar.

"I'm not paying you for this kind of advice."

"Do you feel suspicious about anyone in particular?"

"More than one person, yes."

"Then you're probably narrowing it down. The girl most likely met with trouble at or near that convenience store in Hadwen," Cooney said. "I understand she got into a van in the store's parking lot."

Claire wanted to nod, but stopped herself. How did Cooney know things like this?

"I don't think the girl made a good choice in getting into that van." Cooney gestured to the bartender for another drink. "Some people sell drugs up there, outside the convenience shop, for one. It's best to stay away from those people." The man made eye contact with Claire. "You hear me, Rollins?"

"Yes. I didn't think interviewing those people would be a good idea. Especially Badger."

One of Cooney's black eyebrows shot up his forehead. "A very wise decision, very wise, indeed. Especially if you want to stay alive. Certain people don't take kindly to prying questions. Focus your attention elsewhere."

"I've talked to everyone I can think of and I still don't know who the perpetrator is."

"Talk to people again," Cooney advised. "I make a point of talking to people more than once. If you get my drift."

"Talk? Is that all you do? Just talk?"

"No need to be rude." The bartender brought another glass to the man. "I do the things that have to be done. I'm good at my job."

"Don't tell me anymore." Claire waved her hand at the dark-haired man, and then she turned her eyes to him. "If I paid you, would you be able to find the person responsible for Jade's disappearance?"

"You can't afford to pay me for something like

that." Cooney swiveled and leaned his back against the bar.

"Try me." Claire wanted results. She wanted Bonnie Lyons to have her daughter back, so she would know where her child was, so she could give Jade a proper burial.

"I won't do it," Cooney said flatly.

Claire's eyes widened. "Why not?"

"Because you're capable of doing it yourself." Cooney moved his gaze over the people who had come into the bar. "Who do you think would be useful to talk to next?"

Taking in a deep breath, Claire said, "The new boyfriend, the old boyfriend, and a new flirt."

"Okay, good. I see this case as an emotional thing, a crime of passion, so to speak. Someone wigging out because they can't have what they want."

Claire leaned forward slightly.

"This mess wasn't created by a professional and I'd bet money that it wasn't done randomly or by someone who knew the girl in passing. A lot of emotion was probably involved ... and I wouldn't be a bit surprised if her killer was sorry for what he did. Even if his sorrow is only because he's going to get caught and go to jail." Cooney's attention became riveted on movement at the front door of the establishment. "Well, well."

Claire turned to see a tall, red-haired woman probably in her late forties enter the place. Her form-fitting dress advertised her fitness. She was attractive, and more importantly, alone.

"Looks like this might be my lucky day," Cooney said slipping off the barstool.

"You mean because I came to talk to you?" Claire asked with a sly smile.

"Keep dreaming, Rollins." The man squared his shoulders, straightened his tie, and walked to the woman's table with a warm and friendly smile ... which she returned while gesturing to the chair next to her.

"AJ, I need you to be straight with me." Claire sat with the young man in a small study room in the college library. "You misled me when you told me you walked back to the bonfire with Jade after you and she had been in your apartment. You left out the part about driving around with her."

"I told you eventually." AJ's cheeks colored pink. "And I told you why I left that information out."

"You were afraid it would make you seem guilty," Claire said.

"That's right." AJ pushed his books and laptop to the side of the table.

"But when you lie, you seem even more guilty."

The young man ran his hand over his hair. "I know that now. I didn't know what to say. You caught me off guard."

"Did you tell the police you drove around with Jade?"

"Yes. The second time they talked to me, not the first time."

"You went to Hadwen? You stopped at a convenience store there?"

"Yeah. I needed gas and Jade wanted a bottle of water."

"Did she leave with you?"

AJ hesitated. "No, she told me a friend was coming to pick her up."

"Why? Why was a friend coming? Why didn't she go back with you?"

Tiny beads of sweat showed on AJ's forehead. "We were arguing in the car. I had too much to drink."

"What were you fighting about?" Claire asked.

"She said I was drunk and she didn't feel safe

driving around with me." A sullen expression crossed AJ's face.

"That was the only reason? AJ?"

"Before we got to the convenience store, I pulled to the side of the road. I pulled at her. I kissed her."

"Obviously, she didn't want this from you." Claire's face hardened.

"She told me again she had to break up with her boyfriend first. We argued about it. I started up the car and stopped at the store. She went inside while I pumped gas." AJ let out a sigh. "It was stupid. I've liked Jade for a long time. I didn't want to wait anymore. I reacted in a stupid way. She wouldn't get back in the car with me."

"What about your drug dealer? Was he there at the store?"

"What? Who? He...." AJ flustered and stammered, and then decided to tell the truth. He shrunk in his seat. "Yeah, he was there. He's there a lot. I bought from him that night. Jade had walked away from me by then. She was waiting for her friend at the side of the store."

"What happened then?"

"I drove back to my apartment. That's it."

"What kind of a car does Badger drive?"

AJ looked confused and then what Claire was

getting at dawned on him. "Badger? No, he wouldn't...."

"Tell me what he drives," Claire's voice was forceful.

"He has a few cars." AJ's breathing rate had increased. "When he's selling, he only uses one of them. A van."

Claire's heart dropped. "What color is it?"

"Black."

"What other cars does he own?"

"A black Honda and a black Corvette."

"Any other vans?"

"I've never seen him in anything but the black van." AJ looked like he was going to cry. "I left Jade at the store. Someone.... If I had stayed with her...."

Tears fell from his eyes and dropped onto the tabletop.

You lied to me once. Claire stared at him feeling no empathy. *Are these real tears or am I watching a performance?*

19

Claire and Nicole got in touch with Jade's friends, Alyssa and Cori, and asked if they could meet with them again. They wanted to speak individually with the young women so that one wouldn't influence the other so they arranged to meet at the Whittemore campus center an hour apart.

"Is there news?" Cori's tone was hopeful.

"I'm afraid not." Claire sipped tea from a take-out cup.

Cori looked crestfallen. "I hoped you had some good news for me."

"Can you run through again what happened the night of the bonfire? Starting with when you ran into Jade?" Nicole asked.

"Sure." Cori seemed uneasy, looking from Nicole to Claire as if she wasn't sure what they were after. She told the story of the night from her viewpoint. "I've thought and thought about it. Was I right about seeing Jade walking away with AJ? Was it someone who looked like her?"

"Had you been drinking?" Claire asked.

"I drank a lot." Cori answered sheepishly. "That's why I've been trying to remember things from that night. That's why I've been playing it all in my head, over and over. I don't want to make a mistake. I don't want to be wrong."

"Do you think you remember the night accurately?" Claire asked.

"I don't know," Cori said softly.

"Did Jade call or text you that night?" Nicole asked.

Cori blinked. "I don't think so. Wait. I think she texted me about going to the bonfire."

"After Jade left the park, did she text you again?"

"No, she didn't."

"Did you wonder why she didn't come back to the park?" Nicole asked.

"Um." Cori moved her finger to her mouth to bite on her fingernail. "I guess I didn't. I guess I assumed Jade went home. Alyssa drove her to the bonfire so I figured she probably drove her home. I really didn't think about it."

"Did you see Alyssa at the bonfire after Jade left?" Claire asked.

"I don't know." Cori bit her lip. "I don't know for sure."

Nicole asked the next question. "How did you and Jade get along when you were roommates?"

"Good. We got along good." Cori smiled. "She was easy to live with."

"Were you ever jealous of Jade?"

"No."

"Was Jade jealous of you?"

"No, why would she be? Jade was the smartest, the prettiest, the nicest. All the guys liked her."

"Did you ever argue?" Claire questioned.

Cori shrugged a shoulder. "Sometimes. I guess. No one gets along all the time."

"How did you feel when Jade couldn't room with you this year?"

"I felt bad at first, but then I thought maybe I could get a single room. It's more expensive, but I like living on my own. It's easier."

"Jade texted Alyssa from the convenience store asking her to come pick her up," Claire said.

"But Alyssa didn't see the text until later," Cori

said. "Alyssa texted and called, but she didn't hear back from Jade."

"That's right," said Nicole. "Did Jade try to reach you?"

"I don't have a car right now. It's in the shop. Jade knew that. She wouldn't ask me for a ride because she knew I didn't have my car," Cori explained.

"If Jade couldn't reach Alyssa and you didn't have a car, who would Jade call next?"

Cori's eyes narrowed as she thought about the question. "Probably Kyle."

"But he was in Boston," Nicole pointed out. "He'd have to drive up to Hadwen to get Jade and then take her home."

"It only takes like thirty minutes to get to Hadwen from Boston. It's no big deal." Cori rubbed at her eyes. "Anyway, Kyle was visiting friends at Whittemore. He was only one town away from Hadwen. Jade probably called Kyle to come get her."

"Did you know Kyle was at Whittemore that night?"

"Yeah, Jade told me."

"Why didn't Kyle come to the bonfire?" Nicole asked.

"Jade said he wanted to hang out with his friends," Cori said.

"Did he show up at the bonfire?"

"I didn't see him. There were a ton of people though. He could have been there."

"What did you do after the bonfire?" Claire asked.

"I went back to my room. I didn't feel that good." Cori shifted her eyes to the tabletop. "I had too much to drink."

"Do you know Maggie Burns?" Claire asked.

"Sure. She just opened a hair salon in Bayside."

"You went to school with her?"

"Yeah, through high school. We both grew up in Bayside."

"Are you friends?"

"Not really. We didn't have a lot in common."

"Was Maggie friends with Jade?"

"They were friends." Cori shook her head. "I don't know why, really. They didn't have a ton in common either."

"Did Kyle Vallins go to school with you? He grew up in your town, too, right?" Nicole asked.

"That's right. He was three years ahead of us so we didn't hang out or anything. I knew who he was. I always got the impression he liked Jade, but I don't think he ever asked her out back then."

"Can you think of anything else that might be

helpful?" Claire asked. "Can you think of anything that might help us find Jade?"

Cori shook her head sadly.

ALYSSA, wearing jeans and boots, joined Claire and Nicole at the table in the corner of the student center. She set her backpack on the floor and went to get a coffee.

"I've been exhausted since Jade disappeared." Alyssa removed the lid on her cup and blew on the hot liquid. "I can barely sleep. I have terrible dreams. I have a hard time studying."

"Can you make an appointment with the college counselor?" Claire asked.

"I did. I've seen her twice. It hasn't helped yet, but I have to give it a chance." Alyssa yawned, clapped her hand over her mouth, and apologized.

"We've been talking to people a second time in case something new comes to mind," Claire asked. "Have the police talked to you again?"

"They did a few days ago. I couldn't think of anything new to tell them." She took a careful sip of her coffee. "I thought you might be here to tell me something good." Giving a shrug of her shoulder, she said, "One can hope."

"Someone told us that Jade might have been on the verge of breaking up with Kyle," Nicole said.

"I didn't know that." Alyssa's brow furrowed. "I don't think it's true."

"Kyle told us they were probably headed for a breakup."

"He said that? Wow. I didn't realize. Jade wanted to split up? She didn't say a word about it," Alyssa said, shaking her head.

"She probably didn't want to talk about it until it was decided," Nicole said.

"I had no idea. Kyle always seemed so happy around Jade. He seemed like he really loved her," Alyssa said. "This is a real surprise to me."

"How did Jade seem when she was around Kyle?" Claire asked.

"Jade seemed like she enjoyed his company. If they were planning to break up, it was lost on me. I thought they were a long-term thing."

"Did you ever see them argue?" Nicole asked.

"I don't remember seeing them not get along. Maybe they hid it well. Either that or I'm oblivious."

"When we talked last, you mentioned that you

might have seen Blake at the bonfire," Claire said. "Do you still think he was there?"

Alyssa sighed and leaned an elbow on the table. "I don't think I did see him. I know I'm a terrible witness, but I drank that night ... to excess, so I'm not a reliable witness."

"You missed Jade's text to you asking to come and get her at the convenience store," Claire said.

Alyssa gave a sad nod.

"And when you tried to get in touch with her later, she didn't answer her phone or reply to your texts."

"That's right. I should have been more responsible. I should have seen her text." Alyssa's eyes misted over.

"You were enjoying yourself with friends," Nicole tried to comfort the young woman. "You don't have a responsibility to be tethered to your phone."

"My parents say the same thing to me, but I wish I heard it. Things would have worked out so differently if I'd only heard it."

"Don't blame yourself," Nicole said kindly. "In hindsight, it's easy to say what we might have done. We're allowed to enjoy friends, to go out. We aren't watchdogs. We can't control for everything."

Alyssa nodded, but Nicole could see her words weren't having much of an impact.

"Do you know AJ Phelps?" Claire questioned.

"I know who he is. We're not friends or anything. We were in a class together."

"Did AJ seem interested in Jade?"

"A lot of guys showed an interest in Jade. She was really friendly, so nice. She always seemed happy. People were drawn to her." Alyssa stopped and her eyes went wide. "I guess she drew someone bad to her, too. Anyway, I never saw AJ with Jade. That doesn't mean he wasn't interested in her. Jade and I weren't together all the time."

"Do you have a sense of AJ? What kind of person he is?"

Alyssa looked uncomfortable. "I don't know him well so what I say is only an impression and I could be wrong. AJ seems like the stereotypical rich guy. He has lots of toys. Dresses nice. But he acts unsatisfied. He doesn't seem to appreciate anything, is always looking for a thrill or something new to buy. He's loaded. His parents have everything, but he doesn't seem grateful or thankful for his good fortune. He seems kind of lost, like he has no idea who he is or the kind of person he wants to be. It's only a superficial view of him. I don't really know him."

"If Jade was trying to reach you and she couldn't, who would she call next for a ride?" Claire asked.

Alyssa paused for a moment. "Probably Cori."

"Cori said her car was in for service the night of the bonfire. Jade knew that."

"I think she'd call Kyle then," Alyssa said. "But you said she was thinking of breaking up with him so maybe she wouldn't call him. Not everyone she's friendly with has a car. Maybe she'd call for a cab?"

Nicole and Claire exchanged a look.

It wasn't a cab. It was a van.

"Do any of Jade's friends drive a van?" Claire asked.

"A van?" Alyssa smiled. "Nobody I know here at Whittemore drives a van."

20

Kyle Vallins, Claire, and Nicole sat on the restaurant's outside patio eating lunch under a sunny sky. The young man was fully booked with clients that day and could only promise to meet for thirty minutes before he had to be back at the clinic.

Claire explained that some questions would be repeats from what she asked earlier and what the police most likely asked when they met with Kyle. "Sometimes a helpful remembrance comes to the surface between interviews."

"I don't remember anything else." Kyle bit into his cheeseburger trying to quickly eat his lunch between questions.

"Could you tell us again what you and your friends did the evening of the bonfire?" Claire asked.

A flash of annoyance showed on Kyle's face, but was gone in a second. "It hasn't changed from what I told you the first time."

"We want to be sure we have the correct details." Nicole lifted a spoonful of her tomato bisque to her mouth trying to extend an easy-going manner to help Kyle relax.

With a slight sigh, the man sat back. "I drove up to Whittemore. Met my friends. We hung out in the apartment for a while, then we got hungry and walked to the pizza place on Main Street. After we ate, we went back to the apartment and watched television. Then I went back to Boston. That's it. Nothing exciting. Nothing happened."

"And Jade texted you earlier in the evening?" Claire asked.

"Right. I didn't hear from her anymore after around 9pm." Kyle took long swallows from his water glass.

"Did you run into her at all?" Nicole questioned.

Kyle looked at the woman with a sharp gaze. "I did not run into her."

"You didn't want to go to the bonfire?"

"My friends and I planned the night a while

ago, before anyone remembered there was going to be a bonfire. We talked about going, but we were all lazy and decided to hang around and watch sports."

"Did Jade mind that you didn't go to the bonfire?"

Kyle shook his head. "Of course not. We weren't the kind of couple that was joined at the hip. We got together with friends, we did sports on our own. I like to golf, Jade doesn't, so I go with my friends. She went to a concert and I didn't because we have different tastes in music. We didn't have to be together every moment of the day."

"That sounds healthy," Nicole told him. "What other hobbies do you enjoy?"

For a second, Kyle seemed surprised by the question. "I like to kayak, sail. I ski in the winter. I play basketball."

"Did Jade enjoy kayaking?" Claire asked. "I know she liked the water."

"Jade wasn't a huge fan of kayaking. She thought it was too hard to do in the ocean. She liked boogie boarding. She never learned to sail. I thought I'd teach her sometime, but it was expensive to rent a boat so we never got around to it." Kyle spoke in a matter-of-fact way that didn't reveal how he felt about losing his girlfriend. He kept his emotions in check.

Claire set her fork down on her plate. "You're a friend of Maggie Burns?"

One of Kyle's eyebrows raised ever so slightly. "Yeah, I know Maggie. She recently opened her own salon in Bayside."

"You went to school together?" Nicole asked.

"All through elementary and high school. Jade, too. We weren't always in the same classes, but we knew each other from kindergarten."

"Did you and Jade date in high school?" Nicole asked.

"We started dating the summer after her sophomore year at Whittemore."

"Have you seen Maggie lately?" Claire asked. "Since Jade disappeared?"

Kyle said, "Only briefly. I think it was a couple of days after we found out Jade hadn't returned home. Maggie had just opened her shop. I went by to wish her well."

"Did you stay long?"

"Not long."

The tiny blond hairs on Claire's arms stood up. *Why is he not being truthful? Maggie told me Kyle* had been in the shop that evening for a couple of hours, drinking.

"Did you bring her a gift?" Nicole asked. "A bottle of champagne or something?"

Kyle frowned. "I didn't. I guess I should have brought her a plant or some candy or something."

"Did the two of you talk about Jade?" Claire rested both arms on the table.

"Only a little. I think we both wanted to avoid it. It was too upsetting and she'd just opened her shop and I didn't want anything sad to take away from her achievement."

"Did Maggie get emotional?"

Kyle nodded. "She cried about Jade. I tried my best to comfort her."

"Did you break down, too?" Nicole asked.

"I felt like it, but I held it together. I didn't want Maggie to see me upset. I didn't want her to feel worse."

Nicole reached for her glass of seltzer. "We met Maggie briefly at the town beach a few days ago."

"Oh? What were you doing at the beach?" Kyle asked.

"We went there to look around," Claire said.

"What were you looking for?"

"We wanted to see the place Jade loved. We wanted to see her neighborhood."

"Why?" Kyle seemed dumbfounded by Claire's and Nicole's visit to Bayside.

"To get a sense of Jade."

Kyle blinked, looking confused.

"You like the ocean, too?" Nicole asked.

"Yeah. I grew up around the water."

"Jade's mother said you worked several summers for the lobster tour company. What did you do for them?" Claire asked.

Kyle took another swallow of water. "I did a lot of things, sold tickets, went out on the boat, did some demonstrations of hauling up lobster traps, told some history of the area, handled the boat sometimes. It was a good summer job."

Nicole finished her soup. "Did Jade work for the lobster tour company in the summers?"

"No, she was a lifeguard at the beach."

Claire smiled. "I didn't know that."

"She was a good swimmer," Kyle said. "A lot better than me." He ran his hand over his face. His eyes looked moist.

"On the night she disappeared, Jade texted her friend, Alyssa, to ask her to come to the convenience store in Hadwen to pick her up." Claire ran her finger over the side of her water glass.

Kyle nodded. "I know the place. I stop there for some water or a snack on the way back to Boston from Whittemore."

Nicole sat up. "Did you stop there that night?"

"No. I took a water bottle and a bag of chips from my buddy's apartment. It's only about a twenty-minute drive especially at that time of night. A lot less traffic than during the day."

"Alyssa didn't respond to Jade's message for an hour and a half," Claire said. "When Alyssa finally replied, Jade didn't answer. If Jade couldn't get hold of her friend that night, she must have called someone else. Who do you think that would have been?"

"Cori, probably."

"Cori's car was in for service. Cori said Jade knew that. She knew Cori wouldn't be able to come and get her," Claire told him.

"I don't know," Kyle said. "Did she call a cab?"

"Wouldn't Jade call you?" Nicole asked. "She knew you were at Whittemore. It would be easy for you to go get her."

Kyle's jaw twitched. "There was something wrong with my phone. It kept beeping and then turning itself off. I got sick of it so I turned it off for the night. I went to pick up a new one the next day. Maybe Jade did call and I never got it."

Something picked at Claire. "If she couldn't reach you, wouldn't she have contacted one of your friends?"

"Jade didn't have their numbers," Kyle said.

"What was wrong with your phone? Did the techs tell you why it kept turning off?" Nicole asked.

"I didn't bother bringing it to the store. It was old. I tossed it in the garbage when I got home."

Nicole nodded in an understanding way. "What kind of a car do you drive?"

Kyle tilted his head a little to the side. "A jeep. Why?"

"We're asking everyone the same things," Nicole smiled. "It's only a generic question."

Do you remember Jade saying anything about an argument with someone?" Claire asked. "Had anything unusual happened with someone? A classmate? A friend? A professor?"

"A professor? Like what?" Kyle's eyebrows knitted together.

"A bad grade? A disagreement of any kind? Some sort of romantic advance?"

"No. I don't think so. Jade didn't tell me anything like that."

"How about with someone random? Did she have a run-in with anyone?" Claire asked.

"She didn't say anything like that to me."

"Did she confide that she might be worried about anything?"

Kyle shook his head. "Everything seemed normal."

Claire asked, "You told me earlier that you didn't think you and Jade would continue in the relationship. Had the two of you talked about splitting up?"

"Not really. It was more losing interest in each other. I've been out of school for a while, working. We seemed to be on divergent paths. We hadn't discussed it, but I think we both knew it was coming. It was kind of sad." Kyle bit his lower lip. "And then this happened."

The three sat silently for a minute before Kyle said, "I need to get back to the health clinic. I've already stayed too long. Is there anything else you need to ask me?"

Claire looked the young man in the eyes. "Do you know what happened to Jade?"

Kyle's face flushed. "Of course not. How would I know? If I knew anything, I'd go straight to the police with it. I cared about Jade. I miss her. I want her killer to be caught and punished." Standing up, he stammered, "I need to go."

When Kyle was out of sight, Nicole slowly turned her head to her friend. "He knows something."

"Yes, he does." Claire didn't need paranormal skills to think the same thing. "Is he trying to protect someone, and if he is, who is it?"

21

Claire and the dogs walked the Bayside town beach. Even though the late afternoon had been sunny and warmer, a breeze off the ocean made the air feel chilly. Watching the waves hit the sand and then slide back out, Claire recalled the day when she, Nicole, Robby, and Bonnie Lyons checked under the pier and along the tide line for any tiny clue that could lead to more information about where Jade was. She knew it was basically a fool's errand to think there might be a shred of evidence left behind on the beach despite the movement of the tides and the wind and the people and dogs walking in the sand every day.

Still.

Something kept drawing Claire back.

Such a beautiful spot. How lucky Jade, and her sister, and her mother were to live so close to the beach in the small neighborhood of tidy homes owned by working-class people. Only a few blocks from the Lyons's house, the neighborhoods changed into large homes with huge, sprawling lawns, and a little further away, the grand mansions took up residence on the hills looking down on the sand and sea.

Bear barked at Lady and the two dogs flew along the beach weaving and darting, one leading the way, and then the other one running in front.

A smile played over Claire's mouth as she watched them zip over the beach on their small, quick legs.

A gust of wind ruffled her blond curls and she pushed her hands into the pockets of her jacket. Her gaze moved from one end of the beach to other, finally stopping at the pier and the harbor beyond.

Calling to the dogs, Claire snapped the leashes onto their collars when they'd made their way back to where she was standing.

"Come on, dogs. Let's go see Main Street before the sun sets."

A block away from the beach, stores, restaurants, and shops lined each side of the street and many were decorated with mums and pumpkins. Claire walked the dogs along the sidewalk until she found the place she was looking for, a pretty shop with a red and white awning, window boxes spilling over with pink, red, and white blooms, and a large picture window that looked out over the street. Maggie's new salon.

Claire could see the young woman inside finishing up with a customer. When she opened the door and peeked in, Maggie looked up, recognized the visitor, and smiled.

"Come in," she said.

"I have the dogs with me."

"That's great. They can come in, too."

The last client of the day nodded as she left the salon and Claire led Bear and Lady inside where they greeted Maggie with little tails wagging.

"Such nice dogs." Maggie bent to pat the furry animals and then straightened to lock the door.

"Your place is beautiful." Claire looked over the cream-colored walls, the pretty glass chandelier hanging from the ceiling, the vases of flowers placed here and there, the self-service coffee bar, and the four salon chairs standing in front of an enormous mirror.

"I wanted to create a comfortable, spa-like atmosphere."

"You succeeded." Claire smiled. "It makes me want to sit down and have my hair cut."

"I don't mind staying an hour longer." With a chuckle, Maggie gestured to one of the chairs.

"How are you doing?" Claire asked. "The dogs and I were at the beach for a while so I thought we'd come by to say hello."

"The salon is doing really well," Maggie said. "I have two other stylists starting next week and a nail person coming in three times a week. It's going better than I'd ever dreamed."

"I'm glad," Claire nodded. "Congratulations."

Maggie's expression became serious. "Is there any news on Jade's disappearance? Sometimes, I forget what happened for a second and I look up expecting to see her at the door." She shook her head sadly.

"I don't have any news. I wish I did."

Bear and Lady sat near the front desk looking about the space and then up at Maggie.

"I'm sorry to hear that." Maggie walked to the

coffee bar. "Would you like a warm drink? It's cold outside."

Claire accepted a hot coffee and then she and Maggie took seats in the clients' chairs.

"I was thinking of getting in touch with you," Maggie said. "In fact, after that client that just left, I was going to call Jade's mom to ask if she had your number. It's a coincidence you came in."

"What did you want to talk to me about?" Claire asked.

Maggie sipped from her teacup. "I wanted to ask if there were any updates on Jade. I thought you might know more than what's told on the news."

"I'm sorry I don't have anything to report," Claire said as she and Maggie exchanged numbers. "Give me a call if I can help with anything."

"I'm impatient, I guess," Maggie said. "I hoped there would be some word about Jade."

"Have you seen Kyle Vallins lately?" Claire asked.

Maggie's face seemed to cloud. "He hasn't come by again. Not since he was here right after I opened. He's in Boston most of the time now."

"How long did you say Kyle visited you when he dropped by that evening?"

"A couple of hours. He was very upset about Jade.

He sat in that chair by the sink." Maggie nodded in the direction of the sink. "He was really drunk. He babbled on and on while I finished up my tasks, then I sat down with him and had a few beers."

"Did Kyle drink while he was here with you?"

"He did. He must have downed quite a few before he got here, because his eyes were kind of glassy and he was talking nonstop about Jade. He broke down in tears a few times," Maggie said. "I shouldn't have had anything to drink. It made me feel worse, so depressed and hopeless."

Claire was about to ask something else, when Maggie spoke again.

"I've been thinking about what Kyle was saying." Maggie hesitated and brushed some little pieces of hair from her apron.

A shiver ran over Claire's skin. "Yes?"

Bear walked over to where the young women were sitting, his ears pricked forward.

"He was saying things like *why did it have to happen? Why is Jade gone*?" Maggie rubbed at her temple. "It went on and on and nothing I said could comfort Kyle. I started drinking and it wasn't long before I felt drunk. I hadn't had much to eat all day. I was so busy and I think that's why the alcohol hit me hard. Anyway, I thought it would be best if I headed home and I wanted to call a cab for Kyle. He was slumped in the chair. I had to rouse him. I brought him some coffee, but he wouldn't touch it. He started muttering and he was hard to understand, but it sounded like he was saying, 'I'm sorry. It was a mistake. I didn't want to break up with you.' Like I said, I was drunk, too." Maggie's eyes misted over. "What Kyle was saying made me feel awful. I really don't know why, but it's still picking at me. His words keep playing in my head, over and over."

The lights on the streetlamps flickered on outside the big window and as someone pulled a car to the curb out front, the car's headlights flashed into the shop for a moment.

Maggie's eyes narrowed. "That's Kyle in that car," she said slipping from her seat.

Before she could reach the front door to unlock it, the car sped away from the curb.

"That's odd." Maggie blinked. "Why wouldn't he come in?"

Claire's heart started to race. "Maybe he saw me sitting here and thought I was a client. He probably wanted to talk to you alone."

"Maybe," Maggie returned to her seat next to Claire. "He must have thought the salon would be closed and when he saw someone here, didn't want to disturb me while I was working."

"That must be it," Claire said, even though she thought it was odd that the young man took off so suddenly.

"I wonder what Kyle wanted," Maggie thought out loud. "Just to talk, probably." Shifting to make eye contact with Claire, she added, "I'm glad you were here. I know it sounds awful, but I don't want to talk to him. I felt ... I don't know ... kind of uncomfortable when he was here before."

Lady whined from her position near the door.

"Why do you think you felt that way? Why do you think Kyle made you feel uncomfortable?" Anxiety bounced through Claire's veins.

Maggie frowned. "I don't know for sure. Kyle's sadness, his grief? I couldn't do anything for him. I felt so sad and miserable. I wished I hadn't had those beers. They probably contributed to making me feel worse."

"Did Kyle say anything else when he was here?" Claire asked.

"He talked almost the whole time, but he kept saying the same things." Maggie shook her head and rubbed her hands up and down her arms.

"Have your dreams about Jade stopped?" Claire questioned.

Maggie faced Claire with wide eyes. "No. I keep having them. Sometimes, twice a night." She looked off across the salon and shuddered. "Jade can't reach the surface. She's drowning. It's so terrible. I wake up covered with sweat." The young woman's shoulders slumped. "I wish I could make it stop."

It was late evening when Claire took a break from baking with Nicole and Robby to give Ian a tour of the renovations taking place next door to the chocolate shop.

"They wanted to break the wall down between the spaces tonight, but we told the workers we had to be here for hours after closing tonight and tomorrow night to complete the desserts for the Phelps's wedding," Claire said.

"It will be exciting once the wall is down," Ian said.

"They're going to come in and knock down the wall, then work all night to get the place in shape for the next morning. We'll be able to work and won't have to close the shop. They'll come back on subsequent evenings after we close to do the finish work. It's supposed to take three nights." Claire smiled. "Then it will be done."

"It's going to give you and Nicole a huge space." Ian admired the work that had already been completed. "There will be a lot more seating and this side has the great new kitchen for the catering and for handling the online orders. I think it's going to be a really successful expansion of the business." He wrapped Claire in his arms. "It was a brilliant idea to move beyond the café and go in new directions."

The two shut off the lights and locked the door, and then walked into the chocolate shop.

Claire chuckled. "Soon the wall will be down and we won't have to come outside to get into the other part of the shop."

The backroom was abuzz with Nicole and Robby mixing, slipping pans into the oven, and frosting some of the sweets.

"I see production is in full swing," Ian commented.

Without looking up from his work, Robby gestured to the aprons hanging on the wall hooks. "Grab an apron," he told Ian. "Make yourself useful."

Nicole started one of the dishwashers. "There's plenty to do, if you'd like to lend a hand."

Claire gave Ian's hand a squeeze and winked. "That is, if you don't mind the occasional swearing and complaining when things don't go as planned."

"I'll block my ears." Ian reached for an apron and pulled it over his head. "What are my orders? Make it simple. I don't know how to bake."

Nicole gave Ian some tasks he could handle and in a few minutes, the room was humming with activity and Robby kept everyone entertained by singing some upbeat show tunes.

Before showing Ian the renovations and prior to Robby and Nicole corralling him into helping with the wedding desserts, Claire had spoken to her boyfriend about Jade's case.

"I think Kyle Vallins is trying to protect someone. He lied to me and Nicole about visiting Maggie Burn's at her new salon. He told us he stopped in for a few minutes to wish Maggie well, but Maggie reports Kyle stayed for over two hours drinking beers with her even though he was drunk when he arrived."

"Is Kyle friends with AJ Phelps?" Ian asked.

"I don't think so. Neither one admits to being friends. No one else I've talked to has mentioned that those two are pals," Claire said.

"Do either of them have a connection to the old boyfriend, Blake Rhodes?"

"We haven't found any evidence to support that," Claire told him. "Has your detective friend found anything about a dark-colored van?"

"He hasn't said anything about that."

Claire sighed. "Supposedly, Jade got into a van at the convenience store. She must have called someone she knows to come and pick her up. Or maybe, she ran into someone she knew at the convenience store and asked for a ride."

"From what you've learned about Jade, would she take a ride from a stranger or someone she didn't know well?" Ian asked.

"Her friends say she wouldn't do that. They didn't hesitate when asked."

"See if you can get someone to admit they know a person who drives a dark-colored van," Ian suggested. "The van seems to be the key."

Ian pushed the button to stop the mixer and then he turned to the others with a wide grin. "It looks really good. I did a great job. Maybe I'll quit law enforcement and work here with all of you."

"Dream on, Detective," Robby said as he removed the stainless steel bowl from the mixer.

"What should I do next?" Ian asked eagerly.

Before Nicole could assign him the next task, Ian's phone buzzed and he went to the counter to see the message. When he looked up and made eye contact with Claire, she knew it was something important.

"I need to leave."

Robby was about to tease him about deserting them, but held his tongue when he saw the expression on the detective's face.

With her heart pounding, Claire wiped her hands on a towel. "Has something happened?"

"A man was walking his dog at the Bayside town beach. The dog was at the edge of the water and picked something up. The man thought it was driftwood. He took it from the dog, looked at it, panicked, and dropped it as a wave came in. The object was carried away by the wave."

"What was it?" Claire asked softly.

Ian's eyes were sad. "The man thinks it might have been an arm bone."

Nicole gasped and Robby dropped the spatula he'd been holding.

Claire reached for the table to steady herself as the room began to spin.

Ian said, "My friend asked if I'd come to the

Bayside beach. Lights are being set up. Do you want to come along?"

Claire didn't respond. She couldn't get any words to come out of her throat.

Nicole came up next to her friend. "Go."

Removing her apron, Claire set it on the work table.

Robby brought over her purse and gently handed it to her, and Claire followed Ian out to his car.

CLAIRE STOOD on the sand off to the side to keep out of the way of the police officers and other investigators. Lights on poles had been stuck into the sand several yards apart. Officials hustled here and there and talked together in small groups.

The man and the dog who made the discovery stood near the sidewalk speaking with two officers. Claire couldn't hear what they were saying, but the man looked shaken and upset.

The night was clear and the moon shined a silvery path over the ocean. The waves on the shore sounded louder than during the day.

Even though Claire had on a warm jacket, she

still shivered knowing her sense of the cold was probably exaggerated by the circumstances.

A woman's shouts back from the beach near the street caused Claire to turn around. Bonnie Lyons was being held by an officer as she tugged and pulled and tried to break away from him.

Claire hurried over. "I'll wait with you, Bonnie. We need to let the police do their job. We don't want to get in their way."

Bonnie sobbed. "My baby. It's my baby, isn't it?"

Claire's heart clenched and she put her arm around the woman who suddenly stopped struggling against the officer. Bonnie buried her face into Claire's shoulder and the young woman wrapped her arms around the distraught mother.

An officer found two folding chairs and set them up next to the women, and after fifteen minutes of Claire holding her, Bonnie was ready to sit. Pale and trembling, she sank onto the chair, her hair disheveled and her face pale in the moonlight.

Neither woman spoke … there was nothing to say … but Claire held Bonnie's hand while they sat and waited.

About thirty minutes had passed when a scurry of activity took place at the edge of the water. A man in high boots who had been one of six officers wading in the waves, lifted something from the water and other officers hurried over and clustered together, their heads leaning forward to get a look at what had been retrieved.

A name was called and an older woman came out of the white tent that had been set up and made her way to the group at the ocean's edge.

"They found something." Bonnie stood up and Claire quickly took her arm to keep the woman from advancing.

"Stay here with me. Let them do their work," Claire repeated the words she'd said earlier.

A gray-haired woman wearing jeans and a heavy jacket rushed from the sidewalk and over the sand to Bonnie.

"Bonnie." The woman swooped in and put her arm around Jade's mother's waist. "I only just heard or I would have been here sooner." She looked at Claire. "I'm Bonnie's friend, Sheila. We live on the same street."

Claire nodded and moved away so the women could have a bit of privacy. She wasn't sure if she wanted the object to belong to Jade or not. If it was a bone, then they'd all know that Jade had been put into the water. If it wasn't a human bone, then the mystery of where Jade was would continue. Both options were terrible and the thought of either outcome sent Claire's heart sinking into her stomach.

As a cold gust of wind hit her in the face, Ian came up beside her. Claire knew by the look on his face that there was an answer.

Ian moved close to his girlfriend, put his arm around her, and said softly, "It's a bone from an upper arm. It's human."

A blood-curdling shriek split the night air. Bonnie Lyons had just been informed that the bone was human, and even though it hadn't been determined that it belonged to Jade Lyons, the mother knew. Her tiny shred of hope had been destroyed.

She knew that her daughter was dead.

23

"It must have been horrible." Judge Augustus Gunther sat next to Claire at the small café table in Tony's market.

The early morning light filtered in through the windows and gave the impression that the temperature would be warm and pleasant when in reality, the day was windy and unseasonably cold.

"It was awful. Poor Bonnie." Claire sighed and shook her head. "Poor Jade."

With the Corgis trotting after him, Tony walked by carrying a case of milk cartons. "So finding the girl's arm bone means she was tossed into to the sea to either kill her or to hide the already dead body."

The thought of Jade being thrown into the ocean made Claire's skin crawl. "The police think she was probably dead when the killer dumped her, but it's only speculation right now. They also need to confirm that it is Jade." Her voice held a touch of weariness.

Augustus asked, "Do the police think the young woman was dropped into the sea from the pier?"

"It's possible," Claire said. "The killer might have had access to a boat and could have used that to carry the body."

"Are there any security cameras in the area?" Augustus asked.

"There are some near the yacht club. Other than that, nothing down there would be in a position to capture an image of someone in the harbor on a boat or someone on the pier attempting to dispose of a body."

"Too bad." Augustus raised his coffee cup to his lips.

"What are the police thinking?" Tony asked. "Somebody drove to the harbor, parked, removed a body from the car, and somehow managed to carry the body to the water and push it under?"

"That's what they think right now," Claire said.

"It could be difficult to get the body to the water unseen," Augustus said. "It was late at night, but there may still have been people around. The police go by on rounds, couples or young folks may have been walking the beach or the pier. The killer would have had to be very careful not to be seen."

"It could have been a quiet night," Tony said. "But still ... it would have been easy to spot the killer if he was dragging or carrying a body down to the water. He must have been darn stealthy." The big man went to the cooler case to place the milk cartons inside and the dogs followed him with their toenails clicking on the wood floor.

Augustus set his cup down. "The body would have had to be weighted down in order to keep it from rising to the surface."

A chill ran over Claire's shoulders at the thought of using something to weigh Jade down so she'd sink beneath the water. Did the killer really think he could hide her? Did he really think she wouldn't be found? Maybe he thought his DNA would never be discovered if he dropped the body into the ocean. Shaking herself from her morbid thoughts, Claire agreed with Augustus that weights of some kind would have been required to make the body sink. "The killer had to figure out where to locate a weight. I don't think the murder was premeditated. Maybe I'm wrong. If it wasn't planned ahead of time, then the killer had to scramble to find a weight or he knew where to get one."

"The killer could have a familiarity with the pier or maybe the beach," Augustus said. "He might have known right where to go to get a weight." The older man turned his head to Claire. "Where would someone find a weight like the one that was needed?"

"I asked Ian the same question. He told me the fishermen have lockers down near the harbor and a lot of them have weights in them for lobster traps or fishing lines or nets."

"This killer could have been a fisherman," Augustus observed. "If that was the case, would Jade get into a car with someone like that?"

"Jade may have known some of the fishermen down there," Claire said. "She worked as a lifeguard on the beach in the summers. She might have had contact with the fishermen from being at the beach in the warm weather."

"If she knew the killer, she would have been less worried about accepting a ride home with him," Augustus pointed out.

"And no one around the convenience store reported hearing screaming or noticed a scuffle of some kind. Which makes me think Jade knew the attacker," Claire said, "and entered the vehicle willingly."

Tony walked past the table carrying the empty container that had held the milk. "If the police can find that van, they'll be close to finding out who picked up Jade at the convenience store." He went into the backroom.

"Tony was working up front," Claire said to Augustus. "How did he hear what we were saying?"

"The man must have bionic ears," Augustus rolled up his newspaper. "Either that or he has these tables bugged."

Claire let out a laugh at the idea. "Then he must get pretty bored listening to his tapes of people chatting back here."

"I don't know about that." Augustus's blue eyes twinkled. "Most of the time, we have very stimulating conversations. We discuss the weather, the Corgis, we gossip, we talk about the goings-on in the city."

"The most interesting part of Tony's eavesdropping must be hearing about the dogs," Claire joked.

"I don't need to hear about the dogs," Tony called from the storeroom. "They're usually here with me all day."

Claire's eyes widened in surprise that Tony could

hear what they were saying. She leaned forward and whispered, "He must have supersonic hearing. When did this happen?"

"Perhaps it is some kind of reverse aging of his auditory system," Augustus kidded. "But the rest of him is aging as expected."

"I heard that," Tony said.

AFTER WORKING in the chocolate shop until 8pm, Claire picked up the dogs from Tony, went home, showered, and made some dinner. Now stretched out on the sofa, her eyes were trying to shut and despite the valiant effort to keep them open, the heaviness of her eyelids won out and she dozed off.

The loud *dong* of the doorbell woke Claire with a jolt and the dogs ran barking to the front entryway of the townhouse. Dragging herself off the couch, she went to find out who was calling on her, and when she pressed the button on the intercom, Ian said, "It's me."

When she opened the door, she took one look at her boyfriend's face and knew something was wrong.

"Can you come with me to Bayside beach?" Ian asked.

Claire's breath caught in her throat.

"They've found something. Something has washed up."

"Is it...?" Claire asked cautiously, not really wanting to hear the answer.

"They think it's Jade."

Tears welled in Claire's eyes. "Let me get my jacket."

THE SCENE on the beach was similar to the previous evening with officials buzzing around, a white tent set up, officers keeping gawkers out of the area that was encircled with yellow tape. There was one difference though ... tonight, an ambulance waited at the curb.

Ian was whisked away by his police buddies and Claire was left to watch as long as she didn't get too close. The air was colder than the night before and she was glad she took her heavy jacket.

Ian's friend told her that Bonnie Lyons had been picked up at her home and was now sitting in a cruiser with a social worker who was attempting to comfort the woman.

It wasn't long before a stretcher was removed from the ambulance and carried down the beach to the sand under the pier.

And then Ian left a group of investigators and headed back to stand beside Claire.

His facial muscles tight, Ian said, "It's most likely Jade. They'll take her to the medical examiner's office where they'll make the positive ID."

Claire took hold of his hand.

Ian said, "Hopefully, they can keep Mrs. Lyons away from the body. It's not something a family member needs to see. They can use the dental records to make the identification."

Claire's heart was heavy. "At least, Bonnie has Jade back. That was the main thing Bonnie wanted, to have her daughter back so she could give her a loving burial, so she didn't have to wonder where she was any longer, so she could help her rest in peace."

Ian ran his hand over his face. "It's a heck of a wish for a mother to have."

Claire said sadly, "It's a heck of a world that causes a mother to wish that."

The stretcher was carried up the beach to the

waiting ambulance, the body wrapped in a white sheet. Reporters stood on the far sidewalk, some photographing the proceedings and others interviewing the bystanders. A statement from the police chief would be forthcoming.

Claire bit her lip as Jade's remains were placed inside the ambulance and then driven away.

"We have to find the person who did this," Claire said. "He can't walk around a free man after taking someone's life. He has to be caught. This skill of mine has to be used for good." She closed her eyes and let her breath go slowly in and out, listening to the sounds around her, feeling the cool breeze against her face, trying to sense the things that floated on the air.

And then she made a promise.

I'll find you. You can't hide any longer. I'm coming.

24

Nicole drove the borrowed van along the long, winding driveway with Robby in the front passenger seat and Claire in the back. The desserts had been carefully packed and placed in the van.

"I'm a nervous wreck." Nicole steered the vehicle along the tree-lined drive. "Look at this place. It's ridiculous."

"I'd be happy to live here." Robby admired the landscaping as they drove up the hill to the Phelps's mansion.

"This is the back entrance," Nicole said. "The wedding guests get to go in through the front way. How much money do these people have anyway?"

Claire sat quietly in the backseat watching as

they passed the trees and expansive lawns. "Money isn't everything."

"That's easy for Miss Money Bags to say," Robby smiled.

"You know what I mean," Nicole said. "You don't flaunt what you have. You're gracious, you're generous. You don't shove your wealth in people's faces."

Claire chuckled. "Maybe someday I will."

Robby hooted. "I want to be there when you do that. And by the way, if you're ever looking to share that wad of cash you're storing, I'd be very willing to relieve you of some of it."

"I'll keep that in mind," Claire told him. Robby had no idea that when he ran out of money to pay his college tuition, Claire reached out to the music school to pay the young man's expenses and she made sure she would remain anonymous. Robby thought the school had found a wealthy benefactor to help him out. They sort of did.

The driveway led to what looked like a palace set on acres and acres of lawns. Flowers were planted everywhere and spilled out of urns and pots. A huge white tent could be seen at the rear of the property and arbors covered in ribbons and flowers led the way from the parking area to the white chairs set up for the ceremony.

"Sheesh." Nicole parked the van to the side of the mansion according to the directions that were given to her. "Are we at Versailles, or something?"

A man in a white shirt and black slacks hurried over, checked their names against a master list, and explained where to bring the desserts. Two other men came out pushing wheeled carts and headed to the rear of the van so the sweets could be taken into the house.

Nicole gave the men orders and clucked about being careful with the desserts, and the three bakers followed the carts as they were rolled inside to a huge kitchen at the rear of the mansion.

After looking over the facility, Claire, Nicole, and Robby began to work. They unpacked the items, stored some in the walk-in refrigerators, warmed some pies in the ovens, placed things on platters, and frosted the cakes and cupcakes.

Hearing footsteps out in the hallway, Claire looked up to see Maggie Burns walking past the door carrying a large, caramel-colored briefcase. Maggie and Claire caught one another's eyes, and Maggie entered the kitchen.

The young woman greeted them with a warm smile. "I forgot you were doing the desserts for the wedding."

"What are you doing here?" Nicole asked. "Are you a guest?"

"Gosh, no." Maggie shook her head. "I did the bride's and the maid-of-honor's hair. The bride's usual stylist got sick and someone recommended me so she called me this morning in a panic." She lifted her case. "I should lock this to my wrist. If it ever disappears, I'm done for. It has all of my hair tools in it."

"I understand," Nicole said. "We brought a lot of our own tools, too. Whisks, spatulas, blenders, and two of our professional stand mixers."

After more conversation about their duties at the wedding, the talk turned to Jade.

"It seems the police have found Jade," Maggie said placing her briefcase on the floor and moving her hand to her chest. "There's been no official announcement that it's her, but everyone thinks it has to be. I can't believe it. I expected it, I guess, but to have it a reality is just a shock. I nearly fainted when I heard the news."

Nicole said in a firm voice, "Now it's time to find the person responsible."

"It's not going to be an easy task," Robby said.

A cloud descended over Claire's face. "You're

right. It won't be easy. But, he'll be found eventually."
I know it.

"I should get going," Maggie said and then looked at Claire and gestured to the hallway. "Do you have a second?"

With a nod, Claire stepped into the hall with the hair stylist.

"My dreams about Jade stopped right after the police found the body," Maggie said. "Isn't that weird? I guess it makes sense."

The young woman seemed fidgety and nervous.

"Are you okay?" Claire asked.

Maggie blew out a breath. "You know how I told you Kyle came by the salon right after Jade went missing?"

Claire gave a nod.

"I told you he was babbling. Saying things like *I didn't want to break up with you ... Why did this have to happen?* Things like that. Over and over."

"I remember," Claire said.

"Well. Everything keeps going through my head. That evening in the salon. Kyle drunk. Me getting buzzed on the beer." Maggie pressed her hand against her forehead. "I remembered something. At least, I think I remember it."

"What was it?"

"I think Kyle kept saying *I'm sorry, I'm sorry, I never meant for this to happen.*" Maggie stared at Claire. "I had too much to drink. Maybe I imagined he said that. But, if he did keep repeating that, it sounds bad, doesn't it? Do you think Kyle could have done something bad?"

Claire's heart began to pound. "You're not sure he said those words?"

"I'm not sure. I think he did."

"Have you told the police about this?"

Maggie seemed to shrink. "You think I should? What if I'm wrong? I don't want to get Kyle into trouble."

"I think it would be good for you to tell the police. Tell them what you just told me," Claire said. "Let them decide if it's important or not."

"Okay." Maggie looked down at her briefcase. "I guess so."

"Has Kyle come back to see you?" Claire asked. "He came the evening I was in your shop, but drove away without coming in. Did he stop by again?"

"No, he hasn't. I texted him. He never answered. He must have changed his mind about coming by or maybe he just got busy at work." Maggie let out a sigh. "I'm fine with that. I really don't want to talk to him. He made me uncomfortable. Maybe after some time has passed...."

Claire asked, "That night he visited you at the shop, how did the evening end?"

"Um. We'd finished off the beer. I think I said I needed to lock up and get home. Kyle could barely walk. I told him I was going to call him a cab ... he shouldn't drive home being so drunk." Maggie shrugged. "He refused the cab."

"He drove back to Boston in that condition?" Claire was shocked.

"No, he told me he didn't want a cab. He said he'd sleep it off in his car."

"Did he? Did he go to his car?" Claire asked.

"Yeah. It was parked right at the curb. He got inside, went in the backseat. I assumed he was going to sleep for a while," Maggie said. "I know I'm a terrible friend. I should have invited him to my apartment to sleep on the sofa."

"Why did you decide not to do that?" Claire asked.

Maggie shifted from foot to foot. "I didn't want Kyle coming home with me."

"Because he was so drunk?"

"Because ... I don't know. I didn't like the vibe I was getting from him."

"I don't understand," Claire said.

"I didn't feel comfortable with him," Maggie said. "He was kind of scaring me."

A shiver of anxiety played over Claire's skin. "Why? What scared you?"

Maggie blinked fast several times. "I can't describe it. I didn't want to be alone with him at my apartment."

"It makes sense," Claire agreed. "He was drunk ... you were under the influence. Not a good situation. It wouldn't look good. You were smart not to bring him to your home. You made the right decision."

"I'm glad you think so," Maggie said. "My mind has been a jumble. There's too much going on. Jade. Opening the business. I'm tired. I'm sad. I haven't been able to sleep for days. I feel like I can barely think straight."

"Maybe a day off would do you good," Claire suggested. "Or maybe a half day, if a whole day off from the shop isn't an option. Take some time to relax, rest."

"I should. I'll try. I'd better get going."

"Tell the police what you told me. Tell them what Kyle said to you," Claire encouraged.

Maggie nodded and gave a half-smile. "I'd better

get back. I have three clients coming in later today for me to do their hair for a special function."

"I hope everything continues to go well with the salon," Claire said as she turned to go back into the kitchen. "Maggie?"

Maggie looked back.

"You said Kyle was parked at the curb that night he visited you. He parked his car right outside your shop."

The young woman nodded. "He did, yeah."

"What kind of a car was it?" Claire asked.

"Um." Maggie thought about it. "Oh, it was a van. I remember thinking at least Kyle wasn't in some small car. He'd be able to stretch out in the van and sleep."

Claire's head began to spin. "What color was it?"

"Um. I'm not sure. I wasn't paying attention. A dark color? Dark gray, maybe?"

Claire had to keep breathing deeply to keep her head from spinning. As soon as she returned to the kitchen, she reached for her bag, took out her phone, and called Ian.

25

Claire, Nicole, and Robby got everything done in the kitchen, plated the desserts, and set them out for the servers to deliver to the huge, white guest tent. Music from the ceremony and reception floated into the work space causing Robby to sing as he worked.

"A free concert," Nicole kidded the young employee. "I'm glad I brought you along."

"When the spirit moves me, I can't say no." Robby added a little bit of frosting to one of the cupcakes. "Those wedding guests better enjoy these desserts. They'll never have anything finer."

"Be sure to leave the chocolate shop a glowing review," Nicole gave Robby a playful poke and then looked over to her friend. "Are you okay? You've been very quiet."

Claire washed some spatulas in the sink. "I didn't want to talk about what Maggie had to say until we were finished in here." After giving the details of her conversation, Nicole and Robby stood for a moment without saying anything.

"Kyle? Kyle killed Jade?" Nicole's mouth hung open.

"Kyle didn't really confess," Robby pointed out. "He may have been talking about how their relationship was coming to a natural close. How they were about to break up and now with Jade gone missing, the finality of it all hit him hard. He didn't say he hurt her."

Claire leaned against the counter listening. "Good point. I may have jumped to the wrong conclusion. I think Ian should still pass the information on to his police pal."

"Sure," Robby said. "Have him check it out. It can't hurt and it might lead to a new clue of some kind."

The three bakers finished cleaning up and packed their supplies away. Checking around the kitchen to be sure nothing had been left behind, they filed out of the mansion and headed for the van.

"I would have liked to snoop around. Find AJ Phelps and have another chat with him," Claire said. "But I don't think I'd get very far dressed like this."

Robby glanced at her and agreed. "You wouldn't get anywhere in that outfit. You look like a baker, not a high society guest." The young man went on with his teasing. "You aren't wanted here, Claire. Best crawl back into the van and go home where you belong."

"I don't mind," Claire smiled. "I love home." Settling in the backseat of the vehicle, she checked her phone for a reply from Ian and was disappointed that there wasn't one. She got the idea to send a text to Maggie Burns. *I'm a little worried about what Kyle said to you. It might be best not to let him in if he comes by.*

After waiting several minutes without an answer from Maggie, Claire put her phone back in her bag and watched the scenery as the van made its way down the hills through the fancy neighborhoods. Feeling antsy and concerned, she took her phone from her bag again, but this time placed a call to Maggie. No one picked up.

With a sigh, Claire asked, "Would you drop me

off at the beach? I want to walk over to Maggie's. I want to talk to her. She isn't answering. She must be busy with a client."

Nicole glanced up at the rearview mirror so she could see her friend in the backseat. "So you want to interrupt her in the middle of her work?"

Claire shook her head. "I won't keep her."

The sun was setting and long shadows stretched over the streets and sidewalks.

"We can go over to Maggie's salon with you," Nicole suggested.

"It's okay. Take Robby home so you can get back and relax," Claire said. "I'll take a ride service home when I'm done. No need for the two of you to hang around. I don't know how long we'll talk."

Nicole reluctantly pulled to the curb near the beach. "You sure you don't want us to come?"

Claire opened the door of the van to get out. "No need. Everyone's tired. Head back to the city. I'll text you later."

Before walking one block inland to Bayside's Main Street, Claire glanced at the beach and ocean, and a wave of sadness washed over her remembering the details of the night Jade was found in the water under the pier. She turned quickly away, and strode down the street.

As she made her way along Main Street, Claire admired the shops' fall decorations of mums and pumpkins, and as she passed the lights of the stores and restaurants a golden glow spilled out of the windows onto the sidewalk.

Spotting the newly-carved sign for the salon hanging above Maggie's shop, Claire crossed the street and approached the front of the place, when a feeling of foreboding came over her and her pace slowed. She took a look in the picture window. Only one light was on in the backroom of the store.

Claire recalled that Maggie had three appointments to do women's hair for a gala. Where are they? Why is it dark inside? She couldn't have done all three women's hair so quickly.

Claire knocked on the door, but no one came to open it.

She tried the knob, and to her surprise it turned. She pushed the door open. "Maggie? Are you here?"

The salon was quiet.

"Maggie?" Claire called again.

Nothing.

She stepped in. "Is anyone here?"

Not a sound.

Claire took a deep breath and moved her feet using small steps to cross the space. No one in the waiting area. She came to the door to the workroom, paused, and then walked in to check for Maggie. There was a storeroom to the right and Claire headed in that direction. She put her hand on the knob and turned it.

Except for the supplies, it was empty.

Taking her phone from her bag, she called Ian, but no one picked up. Claire walked back to the front of the store. *Was Maggie mistaken about the three appointments? Did she mix up the days?*

But why is the front door unlocked?

Claire pressed the screen of her phone to place a call to Maggie.

The sudden ringing of a phone on the checkout desk in the shop made Claire jump. *Maggie's phone is here. But where is she?*

Claire's eyes fell on the door on the far wall of the space. The bathroom.

Hurrying towards it, she flung open the door and stepped into the large space.

She stopped and gasped.

Slumped in the corner, sat Maggie, unconscious, her hair falling over her face, her hands clutched against her stomach. Blood soaking her clothes.

"Maggie." Claire choked on the words. Rushing to the young woman's side and kneeling, Claire lifted her phone to call for help when a sound caused her head to spin towards the door.

Someone took a step into the bathroom.

"Hello, Claire." The person in the doorway held a knife.

26

Claire jumped to her feet, her heart banging against her chest wall like a jackhammer. Her vision started to swim. Clenching her fists, she stood straight refusing to panic or pass out.

"You." Claire's eyes narrowed and her jaw set. "Back out of this room," she ordered.

Fifteen feet away from her, the man stared, his eyes wide and his expression blank. A nearly overpowering smell of alcohol poured off of him.

Claire still held her phone in her hand. She didn't think she could hit the numbers for emergency without looking down, and if she did succeed in sending the call, what would happen when the dispatcher spoke over the phone and the man heard it.

"Maggie's hurt," Claire said softly. "She needs help."

The man took a look at the unconscious woman on the floor. "I did it. I hurt her."

"She needs help," Claire tried again. "Kyle. Maggie needs help."

Kyle Vallins looked at Claire with cold eyes. "No."

"She didn't do anything. She doesn't deserve this."

"She knows." Kyle's syllables ran together in a slur.

"Knows what?" Claire wanted to stall for time hoping that Ian had spoken to his friend and the detective would come to the salon to ask Maggie some questions.

"She knows." Kyle's voice got loud. "Maggie knows what I did."

Claire's throat was so dry that she had to force her words out. "What did you do?"

"I hurt Jade."

"How did you hurt her?" Claire asked.

"I was on my way home after seeing my friends at Whittemore. I stopped at the convenience store. I wanted to get some water and a bag of chips before going home."

"Did you go into the store?" Claire moved her eyes slowly around the bathroom trying to spot something she could use as a weapon.

"No." Kyle looked and spoke like a zombie. He swayed a little.

"Why not?"

"I saw Jade there. She was standing outside near the back of the store."

"What happened?" Claire took in slow, deep breaths trying to calm herself.

"I called to her. She didn't recognize the van. My car was in for service."

"Whose van was it?" Claire asked, trying to keep Kyle talking.

"My friend's. He went out of town. He told me I could borrow it."

"What color was it?"

Kyle blinked fast a couple of times and looked at Claire with an expression full of hate. "What? What does that matter?"

"It doesn't," Claire said in a calm tone of voice. "What happened when Jade saw you?"

"Jade came over to the van. She told me she

needed a ride home. She got in. I was going to drive her back to her mom's house."

"What happened on the way home?"

"We talked about the night. I told her what my friends and I did. She talked about the bonfire." Kyle's breathing rate increased. "Then she told me how she ended up at the convenience store." Kyle's face contorted with rage. "It was AJ," he whispered. "It was AJ Phelps. Jade is going out with *me*, but she drove around with AJ." A low guttural sound escaped from Kyle's throat and it sent a cold shiver down Claire's back.

"What did you do?" She kept her voice steady.

"I pulled the van over. I grabbed Jade around the throat. She fought me. I had to punch her. She passed out ... and then I finished choking her."

Maggie moaned from her position on the floor and Kyle took a step towards her, but Claire moved slightly to the left to stand between them and distracted the man with a question.

"Did you put Jade in the water?"

Kyle's glazed eyes looked at Claire and for a few seconds, she didn't think he would respond, but then his mouth opened. "Yes. I knew where the weights were kept for the lobster boat tours. The combination on the lockers was the same. I used them ... to keep Jade in the water. I threw her sneakers in a dumpster. I put her jacket and her phone and her license in a parking lot."

"Why did you do it, Kyle?" Claire asked, the words nearly choking her.

A tear traced down the young man's cheek. "I didn't mean to hurt her. I just got so mad. I didn't mean to kill her."

Claire thought she heard a noise in the salon. Afraid that Kyle would hear it she started to talk. "You need to tell the police. You can't hide from this. They can help you."

Kyle stared at Claire.

"Shall we call the police? We can do it together." Claire lifted her hand holding the phone.

Kyle's eyes blazed and he lunged. "No!"

Claire sidestepped the hurtling man, reached for the room freshener spray sitting on the cabinet near the sink, and as Kyle came at her with his knife, she sprayed him in the face and brought her phone down on the bridge of his nose.

Kyle screamed from the pain in his eyes and as he slammed his lids shut, he grabbed Claire around her neck and lifted his blade above her head.

In desperation, she closed her eyes, hit the spray

button, kicked, and squirmed, and hit the man in the face again with her phone.

Waiting in terror for the blade to strike her, Claire felt Kyle's grip around her neck fall away and he buckled and slid to the floor.

Pushing away from him, Claire scrambled back against the bathroom wall, when she saw someone at the threshold to the room. Her gaze flashed from the person in the doorway to the man on his side on the floor in front of her. A pair of hair cutting shears sticking out of his side.

"Bonnie," Claire gasped.

"Are you okay, Claire?" The woman's body shook violently.

Claire carefully stepped over Kyle and the two women fell into each other's arms.

"You saved me," Claire said over and over. "He would have killed me."

Tears streamed down both of their faces.

Bonnie ran her hand over Claire's cheek. "I'm so glad you're okay. I'm so glad I could help you."

Claire's phone had fallen to the floor in the fight and could not be seen.

"Can you call 911?" Claire asked as she leaned against the wall trying to catch her breath. "Do you have a phone?"

Bonnie made the call, and then Claire handed her a towel she took from the shelf and instructed the woman to press it against Maggie's stomach wound.

Claire held a towel in her own hands and for a second hesitated, before banishing the thought of not helping Jade's killer, and then she kneeled beside the man to try and stop his bleeding.

IT SEEMED like forever before the police arrived along with two ambulances. Maggie and Kyle were hauled into the emergency vehicles and rushed to the hospital. Claire hadn't realized she'd suffered a gash on her shoulder from Kyle stabbing her with the knife and an EMT tended to it. He suggested Claire be taken to the hospital as well, but she refused preferring to wait until Ian arrived.

When he came through the shop's front door and he saw Claire sitting in one of the salon's chairs like she was waiting to get her hair styled, Ian's face crumpled and he rushed to her side. Pulling her into a hug, he buried his face into the shoulder that wasn't hurt. "You need to stop doing things like this. I'm the cop, not you," he whispered.

Claire reached up and ran her hand through Ian's soft brown hair. "I'll try to remember that."

"Where is she?" a young man's voice asked.

"Let us through," a woman demanded.

Claire looked up to see Robby and Nicole pushing into the salon. When they spotted her, they dashed to her side and wrapped their arms around her ... and Ian.

Ian laughed. "Release me and I'll get out of your way."

With tears in her eyes, Nicole looked her friend over, up and down. "You're okay. Thank everything in the world, you're okay."

"I got stabbed in the shoulder," Claire told them.

"It doesn't matter," Robby said trying to lighten the mood. "You've got another one."

Claire noticed Bonnie standing near the door speaking with two officers. One of them gestured to the exit and Bonnie was about to follow him to the squad car when Claire called her name and slipped out of the chair.

"I'm going to the police department to give an official statement," Bonnie said. "My lawyer will meet me there."

The officer looked at Claire. "Not to worry. Mrs. Lyons isn't in any trouble."

Relief flooded Claire's face and she reached for Bonnie's hand. "Thank you. Thank you for saving me."

Bonnie wrapped Claire in her arms and each woman's tears fell onto the other's shoulder.

27

Maggie Burns and Kyle Vallins both survived their injuries and had to remain in the hospital for recovery. Kyle was charged with attempted murder for attacking Maggie and Claire, and he would be charged with the murder of Jade Lyons as soon as the investigation was complete.

Maggie had been in her shop preparing for her clients when Kyle arrived and walked into the salon. Maggie could sense trouble as soon as she saw him. Kyle's expression was angry, his posture and movements were aggressive, and his breath smelled heavily of alcohol.

Trying to remain calm so as not to provoke the man, Maggie edged around the reception desk and took slow steps towards the bathroom, but when Kyle lunged for her, she took off running. Kyle grabbed her from behind just as she reached the entrance to the restroom, they fought, and he stabbed her multiple times. Maggie fell and passed out.

Kyle heard the three clients arriving at the front door, so he quickly closed the door to the bathroom and waited. The women entered the salon and were puzzled by Maggie's absence. After waiting about ten minutes, they decided to leave.

Kyle emerged and went into the backroom to have a look outside at the rear of the building and its parking lot. He decided to move his vehicle from a side road to the back lot in order to carry Maggie out to the car.

On his way inside to get the young woman, he spotted Claire coming down the sidewalk and he hurried to hide in a closet.

When Claire went to check out the bathroom, Kyle made his move to attack her, too.

Claire reported to law enforcement what Kyle had told her about Jade's murder. Ian told her Kyle would most certainly spend the rest of his life behind bars.

A private service for Jade was held one evening

on Bayside Beach and Claire and Nicole were invited to attend. Several of Jade's friends were present, including Maggie who had to use a wheelchair, and both AJ Phelps and Blake Rhodes. It was a lovely service of readings, poetry, music, and the release of a white dove who flew away high over the blue ocean. There wasn't a dry eye in the group.

Bonnie Lyons stood straight and strong surrounded and supported by her friends and her older daughter, Jeena. Both of the woman's wishes had been granted ... her daughter was found and returned to her and Jade's killer had been caught and would eventually stand trial.

Claire didn't know how in the world a family member could grapple with such a tragedy and throughout the service, she desperately hoped that Jade and her family and friends would someday find peace.

"THIS PLACE LOOKS TERRIFIC," Ian said as he admired the Halloween decorations Claire, Robby, and Nicole had put up in the new expanded and renovated chocolate shop. Tomorrow was opening day for the new store, but the friends planned a celebration together for the evening before the big day.

Mums, pumpkins, tiny orange lights, a statue of a black cat, witches' brooms, and cobwebs decorated the space and a long table laden with food stood in the center of the room. The three bakers gave their friends a tour of the new digs and everyone crowed about how great it all was.

Tony and Tessa, Augustus Gunther, Claire and Ian, Nicole and Ryan, Robby and three of his friends, and several new employees and their guests enjoyed the buffet of stew, soups, grilled chicken kabobs, bread, spanakopita, and grilled vegetable paninis, not to mention the festive and beautiful desserts of carrot cake, pumpkin crème brulee, fruit salad, and mini apple cider donuts.

Bear and Lady ate chicken, rice, and cooked carrots from bowls set off to the side, and when they had finished, they licked their lips with long pink tongues and then trotted around the shop greeting the people and accepting pats on the head from the guests who praised the fine dogs for having such good manners and being so adorable.

"It was very fortunate that you encountered Maggie Burns that day on the beach," Augustus told Claire and Nicole. "The young man panicked thinking he had spilled information to Maggie the night he visited her salon and he went back there to silence her. If you hadn't met Maggie, well, the outcome would have been quite different."

"If Claire didn't go to the salon to talk to Maggie," Nicole said. "Maggie wouldn't be alive."

Claire added, "If Kyle hadn't gone to kill Maggie, he still would have been discovered because I told Ian what Maggie reported Kyle babbled about Jade the night he dropped into the salon. And Maggie remembered Kyle was driving a van. The police would have interviewed Kyle and found out he was the killer."

Tony and Tessa joined the conversation.

"It's also a lucky thing Bonnie came to the salon," Claire said. "I think Kyle would have killed me if she hadn't shown up."

"Why did Bonnie Lyons go to the salon that evening?" Tony asked.

"She wanted to talk to Maggie. She heard Kyle had made a visit to her and Bonnie wanted to ask questions about their conversation," Claire said. "And I'm very grateful she did."

Ian came up from behind, put his arm around Claire being careful of her injured shoulder, and looked at her with loving eyes. "And I'm also very glad Bonnie showed up."

Tessa said, "We never know how a small thing we do or a simple decision we make will impact us and the people around us. We should all be mindful of the ripples we send out into the world and try to do the best we can to make those ripples positive, hopeful, and helpful."

"Here, here," Tony said.

The Corgis yipped in agreement.

"Let's have some music. It's time to celebrate," Robby said as his friend turned on the DJ mixing equipment and filled the room with a tune.

Robby and his friends and the new employees began to dance.

Tessa took Tony's hand and led him towards the makeshift dance floor. "Come on, we can show those young people a few moves."

Tony looked apprehensive, but he went along to join the dancers.

Bear and Lady stood on their back legs and began to bounce and twirl in circles to the music.

"Okay," Nicole said as she went to get Ryan. "I'm not going to be outdone by two dogs."

"I will go stand by the young DJ," Augustus said. "I love to learn about new technical equipment."

"Looks like it's just me and you," Claire smiled up at Ian. "We've been abandoned."

Ian touched one of Claire's long curls and took a step closer to her. "I know I've said this before, but please don't let anything happen to you when you're trying to help investigate a crime. I don't know what I'd do without you, Claire Rollins."

With her heart melting from her boyfriend's words, Claire reached behind Ian's neck and gently pulled him in for a long kiss.

"Hey," Robby yelled to Claire and Ian from across the room while showing off his expert dance moves. "I saw that."

Claire and Ian broke from their kiss and chuckled.

Ian smiled at his sweetheart. "Care to join me in a dance?"

"There's nothing I'd like more." Claire took her boyfriend's hand and they headed over to dance up a storm surrounded by their loving friends ... and two sweet Corgis.

THANK YOU FOR READING!

Books by J.A. WHITING can be found here:
www.amazon.com/author/jawhiting

To hear about new books and book sales, please sign
up for my mailing list at:
www.jawhitingbooks.com

Your email will never be sold, shared, or spammed.

If you enjoyed the book, please consider leaving a
review. A few words are all that's needed. It would be
very much appreciated.

BOOKS/SERIES BY J. A. WHITING

CLAIRE ROLLINS COZY MYSTERY SERIES

PAXTON PARK COZY MYSTERIES

LIN COFFIN COZY MYSTERY SERIES

SWEET COVE COZY MYSTERY SERIES

OLIVIA MILLER MYSTERY-THRILLER SERIES
(not cozy)

ABOUT THE AUTHOR

J.A. Whiting lives with her family in New England. Whiting loves reading and writing mystery stories.

Visit / follow me at:

www.jawhitingbooks.com/

www.bookbub.com/authors/j-a-whiting

www.amazon.com/author/jawhiting

www.facebook.com/jawhitingauthor

7-11-21

Made in the USA
Middletown, DE
20 April 2021

37987487R00165